PUZZLE MASTER

PUZZLE MASTER

DISCARD

BY CARLY ANNE WEST
ART BY TIM HEITZ AND ARTFUL DOODLERS

Scholastic Inc.

All rights reserved. Published by Scholastic Inc., *Publishers since 1920.* SCHOLASTIC and associated logos are trademarks and/or registered trademarks of Scholastic Inc.

Library of Congress Cataloging-in-Publication Data available

ISBN 978-1-338-59430-0

1 2020
Printed in the U.S.A.   23

First printing 2021
Book design by Cheung Tai

PROLOGUE

June 7, 1990. Germany.

Have you ever noticed—and I mean, *really* noticed—that trees are kind of like people? That they've got these great, pointy branches kind of like limbs, and they sometimes hold things in them like nests and fruits, and there's a big leafy ball on top, kind of like a person's hair. They come in all shapes and sizes—some are tall, some are short, some are palm, some are elk. And each one has its own story . . . just like us.

Just like her.

Her.

Not her.

It's not her.

My dad's voice reverberates in my brain. *Not her. Not her.*

All around me, there's chaos. People widemouthed and gaping. I spot a curly-haired woman shielding her young son's eyes. And the trees—the trees are in the park, too, standing in stunned horror as they gaze at *not her*, but at the flume ride.

I don't even notice my feet running nearer. I can barely register what's going on. All I know is that I have to get closer, have to find out—how to *help*?

I'm closer to the flume now, closer to the screams, closer to the sound of terror that no one knows what to do with. No one planned for this, I remind myself, though my blood feels cold. That doesn't mean no one saw it coming.

It's not her.

My eyes narrow in on the scene. What must be a coroner walks over with a thick black sheet. The coroner covers a pair of feet with it, then the rest of the corpse. I see just the top of the man's head before the coroner carts his body away.

Not her.

Not her.

Not her.

But him.

A *him* that will never again take a bite of an ooey-gooey chocolate chip cookie, or laugh so hard that water comes out his nose, or cry when the dog dies in a movie. A *him* who will never again run really fast to the bus stop, or tell his family he loves them, or doodle a superhero logo on a piece of paper. A *him* who will never again go to the gym or annoy his little sister or play a video game or read a book.

A *him* whose death will haunt my family across the world, whose life should never have been lost.

A him.

Not her.

It's not her.

* * *

Present Day. Raven Brooks.

I see Dad. While everyone else is in panic mode, he's not. He's looking straight at me. Almost like he was waiting for me. Almost like he saw it coming.

I fall into the unforgiving bulk of his chest. His arms encircle me, but there's a rigidity there, too, one I can't quite place. This time is different from before, the flume ride back in Germany, and I don't know why. Maybe because she wasn't *on* the flume ride last time. But she was now. She was now.

I try to read every part of him. I don't want him to tell me.

It's not her.

I square my eyes and see the front car that has detached from the Rotten Core Roller Coaster, its remaining cars frozen in time at the apex. For so much pain, it looks oddly normal. Like nothing terrible has taken place here. If I pay attention hard enough, I can even hear the squawk of the birds up above—the most normal thing. But this isn't normal. *Shouldn't* be normal. And the shrieks of the people all around us are definitely not normal . . .

I stay for as long as I can in the muffled denial of Dad's chest. But when I hear a wail come from a man in the crowd, I can't take it any longer.

I draw away and look at Dad. Then he says, calmly, as if it was practiced (which I guess you could say it was), "It's not her."

I stare at him hard, blinking back tears. I need him to say it again.

"It's not her."

CHAPTER 1

"**W**ear your blue tie," Mom says, which would be funny if I was in a laughing mood, because I don't own more than one tie. She clicks her tongue and mumbles something about letting out the hem of my pants.

It's not like I've been to a ton of funerals, but this is what I remember her doing before our next-door neighbor Sigrid Keller's wake in Germany. Sigrid used to make us hazelnut cake. But then she got sick and died, and I haven't had hazelnut cake since.

On the morning of the wake, Mom ran around like the most important thing in the world was that we had combed hair and clean fingernails. Like poor Mr. Keller was going to be checking behind our ears for dirt. He didn't come out of his bedroom that morning while everyone left casseroles and cards on his kitchen counter. Not that I blame him . . . but the point is, funerals are not about *me*.

I wonder what Mr. and Mrs. Yi are doing this morning. Because it wasn't *her*—it wasn't my sister, Mya. But it was *her*— their daughter, Lucy. Lucy Yi.

"We leave in ten minutes," Mom says gently from the hallway. She's wearing her gray dress with the lace collar, the one we always tell her makes her look like she lives on a prairie, and she pretends to be mad at us. There are no jokes this morning, though. Nothing feels funny anymore.

Mya steps out of her room in the dark purple dress she wore to *The Nutcracker* two years ago. It's shorter on her now. I remember when the bottom used to drag on the ground, and she'd hold it up until she got distracted by holding popcorn. Now I can see her ankles, jutting out right above her socks.

It doesn't feel right, us wearing these things that we used to smile in. None of this feels right. I guess nothing *is* right.

We make it to the kitchen. Dad's suit hangs over his chair, still warm from when Mom pressed it earlier.

She takes the world's deepest breath, then opens and closes her fists before walking as calmly as possible toward the suit, draping it over her arm, and disappearing into the basement.

Mya and I know better than to follow. We haven't seen Dad since Opening Day.

We each watch the other out of our peripheries, not wanting to make eye contact, but also not wanting to miss the smallest look, the vaguest sign of how we should behave, what we should be feeling, how we were going to manage this.

After a long spate of silence, Mom's footsteps ascend the stairs, thumping a little harder than they had on the way down. She's still carrying Dad's suit over her arm though he's nowhere in sight.

"It's time to go," Mom says.

Mya and I stand still.

Mom tosses the carefully pressed suit over the back of the sofa and turns to us.

"I said let's go."

There will be no discussion. We follow her to the car.

On the drive to the Raven Brooks Home of Eternal Rest, we are silent. I watch Mya fiddle with the gold bracelet around her wrist, her Golden Apple charm tipping backward and forward on its loop.

Mom parks the car at the far end of the lot. We walk in a line toward the funeral home, where a woman dressed in crisp black trousers and a cream-colored blouse waits at the curb to give us each a program.

It's a list of everything we're supposed to do to say goodbye to Lucy.

I try to look around at other people's faces once we enter the funeral home, but they all have their heads down. They seem to be looking at the program, too. I wonder if they're glad to have instructions, or if they think it's strange that there's a schedule. Maybe, like me, it's both.

Aside from the woman out front, Mrs. Yi is the next person to greet us at the funeral home, which I didn't expect.

"Mya, Aaron," she says, enunciating each syllable in our names as if we're the Duke and Duchess of Cornwall. "Diane." There are no hellos here, though—just an acknowledgment.

Raven Brooks
Home of Eternal Rest
In Memory of Lucy Yi

Welcome
A Hymn
A Song
A Tribute to Life
A Eulogy – Family
A Eulogy – Friends
A Song

I don't think Mom knows what do, because she blurts, "It's so awful, Brenda. It's just so awful."

This is not the mom who organized a food committee for Mr. Keller in Germany, ensuring he had a hot meal every night for the entire month, who sorted his mail and asked him quiet questions, never more than were necessary.

"Thank you for coming," Mrs. Yi says, and even though it's the right thing to say, it sounds somehow wrong.

It takes me a second to understand it's because she doesn't want to be saying it. Not to us.

I look at Mom for answers, some indication that we're supposed to be here, that everyone in Raven Brooks doesn't wish it had been one of us instead.

But Mrs. Yi is already greeting the next person, and Mom is already walking to a pew at the back of the room, and Mya looks like she's lost her way completely.

Suddenly, I feel Mya's hand slip into mine, and I have the answer I'm looking for. We are *supposed* to be here. Lucy was our friend.

There's a folded *Raven Brooks Banner* left abandoned on the pew beside me, and I try distracting myself with the crossword, but I feel like everyone's watching me. I push the newspaper aside, barely taking note of the blocks of letters that spell part of an unintelligible sentence:

follow the crows

7

Then the procession begins.

Mrs. Yi is the first to speak, and I think maybe she's super-human because I can't understand how she's even standing. I know *I* feel like a pile of mush. Then I hear Mr. Yi sobbing from the hallway. He couldn't even come in the room with all of us. I think I get it; Mrs. Yi is superhuman because she has to be. Because, thanks to the amusement park ride, she doesn't have a choice.

In the shadow of my eye, I realize that our friends Enzo, Maritza, and Trinity, and their parents have sat in a row behind us, all of them lined up, heads down. I try to make eye contact with Enzo, my best friend, but his gaze doesn't meet mine. I want to go over there with them, but I can't help but shake the *otherness* that I feel. Like we're not supposed to sit with them.

A lady Mrs. Yi introduces as Lucy's Aunt Beatrice plays a song on the bassoon.

A man Mrs. Yi says is their pastor says a prayer from behind the dark green coffin.

I try to listen to what every single person says as they take their place behind the green coffin and the flowers. I want to hear how amazing Lucy is, how much she made music club something people wanted to join, but my stupid brain can't stop wondering what Mrs. Yi is going to do when she gets home and has to stare at a thousand casseroles on her countertop.

When the service ends, people file out of their pews one by one, but they aren't leaving through the back door, where we all entered. They're leaving through a door at the front of the hall.

8

And they're stopping at the green coffin, one after another, pausing.

Stopping to say goodbye to Lucy.

Mya must have just realized it, too, because she's squeezing my hand again.

"I can't," she whispers, her voice cracking.

I don't know if she means she can't believe what's happening or she can't see the casket. Or maybe she can't do this anymore. Either way, I can't, Either way, I can't.

"We have to," Mom says now, her voice calm and smooth, as if she's talking about the tuna fish she ate for lunch. And I know she's right—it's not about us. It's about Lucy.

"C'mon," I tell Mya, holding her hand between both of mine. "I've got you."

There are what must be one hundred flowers draped over the green cover. The casket doesn't look long enough to fit her. Was Lucy really that small? A wave of panic pours over me as I picture her curled up, struggling to stretch her legs.

"It's okay," I say to myself, but Mya thinks it's for her, and she squeezes her fingers tighter around mine.

Mom goes first, and with one hand clutching a crumpled tissue, she reaches her free hand to the casket. Then she seems to think better of it, stopping her hand in midair.

Someone in the pews behind us coughs.

Mom sniffs hard before stepping aside for Mya and me. She's waiting for us. Everyone is waiting for us.

Then I hear someone say, "He didn't come."

To which someone else replies, "Would *you*?"

They weren't whispering. We were meant to hear it.

Brenda Yi's words circle my brain like a draining sink. *Thank you for coming. Thank you for coming. Thank you for coming.*

But she isn't thankful. Why should she be? And why would anyone else? My dad built the machine, the amusement park ride, that killed Lucy. That resulted in her untimely death. The cursed Peterson family brought tragedy and fear back to the town we haunted for a generation.

I don't remember how I get outside, but out of nowhere, the sun makes my vision go white, and I can feel the heat of it on my neck, unrelenting. I squeeze my hand and realize that it's empty. Mya isn't holding it. After a second, I hear the click of my mom's heels on the pavement.

"I think it's best we go," she says, her voice thick.

Then Mya is there, standing between Mom and me, her eyes dark.

"The reception is next door," Mya says.

"We're leaving," my mom replies. I expect Mya to be relieved, almost, but neither of us is prepared for her response.

"We can't! The reception—"

"Mouse, I don't think anyone wants us—"

"I don't care! She was my friend!"

Mya is holding her little gold bracelet like it's the most important thing in the whole world.

I can tell this isn't enough to convince Mom, who looks like she wants to get out of the funeral as fast as she can. I look at the two of them and realize that out of the three of us, I'm the deciding vote. *Sigh.* Usually I'd side with Mom, but Mya needs me more now. I breathe in and out real slowly, just like Mom's *Pilates for Ladies* books tell ladies learning Pilates to do.

"I want to stay, too," I say.

There is nothing I want less than to stay for one more second, to hear one more whisper, to dodge one more look.

But this?

This is for *her.*

"Okay," Mom says. "Okay."

The reception hall next to the Raven Brooks Home of Eternal Rest says it's available for SPECIAL OCCASIONS! WEDDING RECEPTIONS, CHRISTENINGS, BAR MITZVAHS, RETIREMENT PARTIES, AND CORPORATE FUNCTIONS!, but its geographic location seems to pretty much keep it occupied with matters of death. When we enter, I hear the funeral home director and reception hall hostess make friendly conversation.

"Lunch next week?" the director asks. "Lasagna? Or moussaka. Something with layers."

I can feel my hands get clammy. Next week seems like a lifetime away, but for them, it's just another funeral for someone who probably hasn't even died yet.

We make our way to the bustle of the reception hall. Trinity finds me before anyone else. She looks almost totally normal, except for a little puffy pink line beneath her eyes.

"Aaron, I'm sorry," she says, and I think I see the puffiness a little heavier now. "We wanted to sit with you at the funeral, but that awful grocery store woman cornered my parents."

I shrug. I think I know what Trinity means. Mrs. Tillman, the

11

owner of the Natural Grocer, cast some terrible glances my way during the funeral. She probably thinks I killed Lucy.

Enzo follows closely behind Trinity with his little sister, Maritza, in tow, all looking uncomfortable in their formal outfits. The sleeves on Enzo's shirt are too long on him, and his tie is disjointed.

"Ties. I don't understand ties," Enzo grumbles. "Like, who decided a *tie* is the pinnacle of 'special occasion'?"

Special occasion. I think back to the sign. WEDDING RECEPTIONS, CHRISTENINGS, BAR MITZVAHS, RETIREMENT PARTIES, AND CORPORATE FUNCTIONS!

"Maybe we should check out the food," Enzo adds, trying to change the subject.

"I think there's a little salami," Trinity says, and apparently "salami" is the magic word because we line up at the buffet.

Only when one of the people in front of us moves do I see who it is: Detective Dale.

Detective Dale, the same cop who has had it out for me since I started investigating my grandparents' weather station. You see, my grandparents had a weather station here in Raven Brooks, and that's why my dad moved our family here after Germany proved to be too painful. But it wasn't just a weather station, it held secrets—secrets I haven't even scratched the surface of. And I'm determined to find out.

I suppose it makes sense that Detective Dale would be here, respects to pay and all. But he doesn't appear to be offering a single condolence to Mrs. Yi, who is sitting in a chair swarmed by people offering her cakes and cards and phone numbers and hugs, all of which she takes, none of which she seems to want.

Instead, Detective Dale listens tiredly to Mrs. Tillman, who peers over his shoulder, and piles his paper plate high with all the cured meats his chubby hands can get on. I pretend to reach for a toothpicked gherkin, though really I'm just listening in.

"Detective Tapps, surely you can understand the anguish the good people of Raven Brooks feel over this entirely avoidable tragedy," Mrs. Tillman says. "And I'm quite certain you appreciate the catastrophic impact this has had on the community, especially after all that's known about the . . . the *persons of interest* involved in the matter."

"Yes, but I'd caution you to—"

"Detective Tapps, believe me, no one has more empathy than I do . . ."

I hear a snort behind me and only just now realize that Enzo's been pretending to reach for the same gherkin that I have.

"Oh yeah, she's a real Mother Teresa," Enzo mutters.

I feel a warmth spread through me that I haven't felt since before Opening Day.

"I can assure you, Mrs. Tillman, we're doing everything in our power to conduct a thorough investigation," Detective Dale says, and in that moment, his eyes scroll the room and land right on me.

I think for a second that he might come over to speak with me, and I can feel my hand starting to shake the contents of my plate. Then, seemingly out of nowhere, Mrs. Tillman is unceremoniously shoved aside by someone larger and apparently more worked up than she is.

"Isn't that the former Channel Four guy?" Trinity whispers.

There he is, Gordon Cleave, looking barely recognizable since the last time I saw him, which was, what, five days ago? I guess if I look rough, this dude looks *bad.* Yet the events of that morning almost a week ago somehow feel like a lifetime ago—the path I cut through the woods and into the tunnels to catch him in the act, the fall through the Observatory door right into the menacing hands of a man standing mere feet from me now, looking so much less threatening without his powerful job and pocketful of secrets. A Forest Protector in the flesh, looking more like a plucked bird today.

Something has changed, something major. But I have no idea what.

What I *do* know, though, is that his stare might vaporize me right here where I stand. He's holding Detective Dale's arm tight enough to make Detective Dale wince, and Mrs. Tillman looks like she's about to knock over the whole pile of prosciutto, but none of that can deter Gordon Cleave from the death stare he's got me locked in.

"Dude, why does he want to melt you?" Enzo says, noticing what's impossible not to notice.

"A lot of reasons, I guess," I say, which isn't wrong, but something else is going on. Something happened that day in the Observatory after I left, something after Lucy.

Gordon Cleave leans into Detective Dale and murmurs something in the detective's ear. Only this time, Detective Dale looks worried.

And angry.

Now they're both looking at me.

"Whoa," Enzo says. "Did you, like, smash his vintage action figure or something?"

Just like that, the memory returns of Gordon Cleave fishing in his pocket, a panic spreading across his face when he realized whatever he was looking for was gone.

"Yeah . . ." I say, unable to escape the feeling that the answer is right in front of me, but I still can't see it.

I guess there's nothing else to do but eat, so I help myself to a few more gherkins and slivers of salami, as a treat. After an hour or so has passed, Mya and I follow Mom out of the reception hall and into the parking lot, just as much at a loss for words as we were when we were walking in the other direction.

In the car, Mya leans her head against the window, staring at the back of Mom's seat. Mom, though, keeps glancing out the rearview mirror, which I wish she'd stop doing because she's veered into the opposite lane twice now, narrowly missing oncoming traffic.

"Mom?" I say after the second near miss.

"Sorry," she says, still distracted. "It's just . . . that black car . . ."

I turn in my seat to get a look at the sedan behind us, but all I can see is a white-haired lady in a Cadillac. She's just red eyeglasses and a poof of curls struggling to see over the steering wheel.

"I don't see any black car."

Mom shakes her head. "It might have turned," she says, her voice far off. "I just would have sworn I saw it earlier this morning. And then at the reception . . ."

At last, Mom peels her gaze from the mirror and focuses on the road. I try to believe whatever she saw was nothing, but I can tell she doesn't believe it, and frankly, I'm not sure I believe *anything* anymore.

Once we're home, I focus my attention back on Dad. I tried my best to ignore it, but where *was* he during the funeral? He knew Lucy just as well as Mom did.

But the house is dark.

I'm not even sleepy, which makes no sense considering I've barely slept since the accident. My bed calls to me anyway, and maybe I just want to lie there, stare at the ceiling.

Yet when I get to my room, I can tell immediately that some-one else has been there.

Nothing is disturbed or disorderly; however, the one place I thought was sacred—the hidden panel behind the middle drawer of my desk—isn't how I left it.

"No. No, no, no, no, no, no," I say, ripping the drawer from its hinge.

"It's not possible!" I say, but I already know it happened. The one place I thought would be secure—the single place I thought I could hide my grandparents' notes—has been compromised, and their notes are gone.

Without thinking, I fling my bedroom door open and barge into Mya's room, ready to relay the news. I enter so brashly, it never occurred to me that I'd find her curled beside her bed, head in her arms, knees soaked with tears and snot. And even though I can feel the heat of the moment in my cheeks, I realize I have to set it all aside *this second* to be the big brother that Mya needs right now.

"What happened?" I ask her.

Everything has happened. How could I ask that? But this sight of Mya is one I wasn't ready for, and her face is so red, and her eyes are so swollen . . .

"It was supposed to be me," she says, her voice small.

"What?" I don't know what Mya means.

"It was supposed to be me," she repeats, her voice so thick, she doesn't even sound like Mya. "It was supposed to be me in the front on that awful ride, Lucy and Maritza in back. It wasn't

17

supposed to be her in front, but my legs were too long, and she cried because she didn't want to, but I said it would be fun. *I said it would be fun.*"

Mya's head falls back into her arms.

It takes my stupid brain several more seconds to understand.

It was supposed to be Mya in the front car. Mya. It wasn't supposed to be Lucy who died.

It was supposed to be my sister.

It's not her.

I hate that I think this, but instantly my mind swaps the funeral for Mya's. *Mya's funeral.* Mom stands in front of everyone, thanking them for being there, while Dad is inconsolable outside. Nosy Mrs. Tillman is sitting in the back row, muttering on and on about how she always took pity on us Peterson kids. I'd have to get up there and give a eulogy and pretend like Mya and I didn't fight over rice cereal every other day. *Mya's funeral*—I can't believe I'm thinking it. I try to get those thoughts out of my brain.

There's nothing else to do but hold her.

"It wasn't your fault," I tell her.

Mya doesn't stop crying. I can tell she wants to be alone, so I return to my room. I wanted to tell her about our grandparents' notes, but I think that might be too much for her to handle right now. And who could blame her? It's hard enough that your friend died, or even that people blame your dad for it. It must be really hard to blame *yourself,* too.

I do what any normal kid does when they can't sleep. I stare out the window. Everything outside is normal, if normal is even a thing anymore . . .

Until I spot what must be the same black car Mom saw earlier.

Its lights are off, and I can't tell if there's anyone in it, but I know two things for certain. One, it shouldn't be there. Two, I've never seen it before.

Yet there it is, parked right in front of our house.

CHAPTER 2

The big news of the day is that a new monument has gone up in the Square, the main hub of our town of Raven Brooks.

"Have you seen it?" Maritza says, her nose scrunched up like she smells a raccoon fart. "It's basically a Golden Apple Corporation advertisement. Lucy's plaque is practically invisible."

"They spelled her name wrong," Trinity sighs.

"Did you really expect them to honor Lucy?" says Enzo with a level of jadedness I've never heard from him before. "They've been saying it before the amusement park was built—Golden Apple will bring tons of tourists, tons of money, yadda yadda. Of course they'd want to downplay that something terrible happened here."

"My dad says the company is on the verge of bankruptcy," Trinity says solemnly. "They sunk everything they had into the Golden Apple Amusement Park."

"Mmm," Maritza says, and we're all quiet for a moment.

I can't help it. I blurt it right out.

"I'm being followed," I say.

Maybe it's because I couldn't sleep. Maybe I'm just rattled by the monument. But my confession comes out all wrong, and now I've broken the silence so awkwardly, I have to explain.

Lucille Morgan Yi, Gone too soon.

"Don't freak," I start out. "But I think a car followed us home yesterday from the funeral."

Mya shrugs. "I think Mom said something about it."

"She did. And then I saw it again last night, parked out in front of our house."

Mya cocks her head, a look of genuine confusion. "Seriously?"

"I don't know," Trinity says, ready to dismiss the whole thing. "They probably live on your street. It's just a car."

"But I've never seen it before," I protest. "It's . . ."

Now Maritza is shaking her head. "Aaron, you saw the same car twice. A normal old black car. Raven Brooks isn't a big town. I'm sure if we all paid attention, we'd see the same cars around, too."

There's something different in her voice, and if I'm being honest, I'm taken a little aback. Is it . . . pity? No, not exactly. More like . . . fatigue. Like she's tired of having to explain things to me.

Normally, I feel like I can talk to my friends about anything and everything. What's all this about?

She's still processing what happened to Lucy, I remind myself. *We all are.*

I take a deep breath. That must be it. I harken back to when Mrs. Keller died and the town felt solemn for a while. "Everyone processes grief differently," Mom had told me. "And every process is valid."

But Maritza is not the only one who looks a little fed up. Trinity and Enzo seem less willing to entertain my suspicions, too. Suddenly, I feel like I have to defend myself to my friends.

"What if it's Mr. Cleave? And what if he's after me?" I say, reminding them how I found Gordon Cleave clutching his Forest Protector robe in the Observatory not too long ago. Who knows what the news reporter was doing, but it definitely wasn't good.

"Aaron," Enzo says. His face is blank, like I can't quite read it. Or maybe it isn't blank but it's written in a language I just don't speak. "This week has been awful."

Trinity nods. "The worst."

"We're all just trying to deal," Enzo continues, using a tone that makes me feel like I'm a baby.

"Yeah, I know," I say, maybe a little too defensively.

Mya's caught on, though.

"Guys, our mom saw it, too," she jabs.

Trinity, Maritza, and Enzo exchange an almost imperceptible look. Then Trinity says, in a voice much smaller than I'm used to, "How, um . . . how are your, er, mom . . . and dad . . . doing?"

I don't understand at first, not until I see Mya's face fall. Mention of my mom made them wonder about my dad. Just like everyone is wondering about my dad. About why he didn't go to the funeral.

"They're . . . you know . . ." I start to say, though I'm not sure how I'll finish the sentence.

"Good," Trinity says, nodding vigorously, like my answer actually *answered* anything. "That's good."

What does she expect me to say? *Well, you see, my dad hasn't left the basement in almost a week, and yes, I realize that makes it look like he's responsible for the accident, but he couldn't be. Not really. Right?*

I think back to yesterday, to the funeral and our lonely pew of three, our friends with their heads bowed, and their eyes refusing to meet ours.

It feels like life has suddenly split into two parts—before the accident and after. Before was the mystery of Forest Protectors and discoveries in the tunnels that connect my house to the Weather Station, to the Observatory, the Factory. Before was notes from my grandparents to decipher and the hope that they were framed for crimes they never committed. And now there's After. I'm not even sure what's in the After quite yet.

Those events feel so far away now, like they happened in a different lifetime. And no one seems eager to revisit any of it. No one but Mya and me.

"You know what you need, Aaron?" Enzo says suddenly, sharply. "A hobby."

I sigh. "Not this again."

"Just hear me out."

There's no hobby in the world that will change any of this. Especially not the one I know that Enzo is going to suggest.

"Enzo, no offense, but I have zero desire to work at the *Raven Brooks Banner*," I say. "It's awesome that you do it. Really! It's, like, your *thing*."

Enzo crinkles his forehead. "My thing?"

"Yeah! You know. You've found your thing—your calling, whatever. It's a thing that makes you happy."

"You think I'm happy with . . . the news?" Enzo says, his forehead wrinkling.

Okay, that's not what I meant.

"Not like that." I try a recovery. "What I mean is, it's great that you found, er, a *hobby*, but—"

"All I know," Enzo interrupts, "is that I hear the gossip first, and if I'm lucky, I get to *see* it first, too," Enzo says, then meets my eyes, "and that's all wonderful, but I was thinking, it'd be even better if I had a buddy to hang out with."

A buddy? I can honestly say I'm surprised. And actually, a little touched. I guess it *has* been a while since we got to hang out, just the two of us. But then there's a creeping suspicion in the back of my brain . . . it never seemed to bother Enzo before that he didn't have a friend at the *Banner* to swap stories with. And if he was so concerned about hanging out with a buddy, why wouldn't he just invite me over for dinner?

"C'mon," Enzo persists. "With Channel Four imploding, my dad's going nuts. Being the editor is serious business. And everyone knows you, and everyone knows you have an eye for cool investigative stuff."

"I've got a lot going on right now," I say, which isn't untrue. Let's see: a mysterious black car, a dad who won't leave the basement, two individual theme park accidents resulting in two different deaths . . . Honestly, it's a full-time job just being a Peterson, and I can't even bill overtime.

Being a Peterson: 70 hours a week.

Overtime: Not eligible.

Enzo and Maritza exchange a look. I can almost hear them asking who's going to tell me first.

"Just say it," Maritza sighs, giving her "you'll never win this one" glare to Enzo.

He takes a deep breath. "All right, I wasn't going to mention this," he says steadily. "I mean, it's not like you need any more reasons to be paranoid these days."

Yeah, those are *exactly* the kinds of words that make me more paranoid.

"Dude—"

"But," he cuts me off, "you know how my dad hired a new crossword maker, right?"

"How would I possibly know that?"

"Oh. Well, we hired a new crossword maker," he says.

"Congratulations. You must be very proud."

"The thing is, nobody knows exactly who the crossword maker is," Enzo says. He catches my bemused stare. "Dad's got a special way of communicating with him. Anyway, that's not the point. The point is, well, ah . . . he sort of . . ."

"What?" I say. The suspense feels a tad unnecessary. Aren't we all tense enough as it is?

"The Puzzle Master asked for you by name."

He might as well be waving a bright red flag right in my face.

"Care to elaborate on that creepy little detail?" I say.

"No, no," Enzo says. "It's not like that. See, his puzzles are getting more complicated, and apparently, people love not being able to solve puzzles, so Dad keeps having to make more room on the page. Now he's looking at making the puzzles *two* pages

25

every issue, but the Puzzle Master doesn't have time himself to make another puzzle every week . . . Anyway, long story short, the Puzzle Master told Dad that he'd seen your work, and that you have a good eye for design. And he, er, asked for you. For your help."

"My . . . work?" I repeat.

"I know, right?" Enzo laughs. "I mean, what's he, like, visited the exhibition in your basement or something?"

I can't explain it, but mention of the basement—my dad's office—feels like a dig somehow. I know I'm not being totally fair. After all, Enzo doesn't know the basement is where my dad has been holed up lately. And maybe he wasn't thinking about all the tunnel exploration that started and ended in that very same basement, the exploration he doesn't even bother to mention now that there are other things to focus on besides clearing my family's name. But *I'm* thinking it.

Enzo slides the most recent issue of the *Banner* into my hands, and I immediately recognize the puzzles page that he has the paper folded to show.

It's the same one that was sitting on the pew beside me at Lucy's funeral, the one whose answers spelled out **follow the crows**. Only this one is entirely filled out, and the way it's turned in my hand, I read a new phrase I couldn't have seen before: **to find the Ravens**. Unconsciously, my brain strings the phrases together.

Follow the crows to find the Ravens.

It feels like more than a coincidence, and somewhere at the edge of my brain, I feel a tickling. It's like an itch I can't reach to scratch, a sneeze I can't sneeze, a fever I can't sweat.

But now I have no choice. I need to know more. Could the Puzzle Master hold the answers I've been looking for?

"I'll do it," I say, the words toppling out of my mouth. "A . . . hobby, yeah? Maybe it does sound good. To get my mind off . . . all of this."

We both know that's not why I agreed, but neither of us presses it.

"Oh! Um . . . awesome," Enzo says.

"Cool," I reply.

"Cool," he says.

* * *

On the way home, Mya holds her tongue for a whole three minutes and twenty-five seconds.

Then she whispers, so softly that Mom can't hear, "You should tell Mom about it."

"About what?" I say, as though it isn't occupying my every last thought. "The *Banner* gig? Nah, it's fine. I'm sure Mom has other things to worry about."

"Riiiiiight," Mya says. "So you don't find it at all strange that this Puzzle Dude asked for you by name, that nobody knows who he is, or that you actually agreed to do it?"

Mya's a dog with a bone.

"Puzzle Master," I correct her. I can tell that answer isn't helpful, though. "Mouse, listen. What if the Puzzle Master has something to do with, you know, *everything*? With the Forest Protectors and whatever Grandma and Grandpa were onto?"

Mya scrunches up her face. "Seems like an awful lot to put on some mysterious puzzle maker," she says.

I shrug. "If there's even a chance it could help us get to the bottom of whatever the Forest Protectors are doing, maybe it can . . ."

Maybe it can clear Dad's name. I don't need to say it. Mya knows. I can tell in the way she doesn't ask me to finish.

Ah, there it is, buried under the debris of the accident—that tiny spark of hope. Hope that there might still be a chance for us Petersons, to explain all the horrible wickedness that's run amok in Raven Brooks.

When we pull onto our street. Mya gasps first. Or maybe I do. I'm not sure.

A black car sits directly in front of our house.

CHAPTER 3

Two men in suits are in the car. When Mom sees them, she smiles, almost like they're old friends. "Would you like to come inside?" she asks. "It's a nice day for some tea."

It's actually very hot out—unusually hot, if I'm being honest—and not really the weather for tea. But I guess the men in suits and Mom think it is, because they follow us into the house without saying anything else.

Mya and I exchange a look. It says, *What is going on?*

Mom makes sure the guests are seated and brings out an old tea set. She hasn't used it since Mya borrowed it for a tea party gone wrong in Germany with a bear and a doll that will remain nameless. Mom was mad but Dad played along. He got *really* into it, too. He wore a clown suit, complete with that poofy hair and red nose, and whenever Mya served tea, he'd shout, "STOP CLOWNIN' AROUND!"

Suffice it to say the doll was poisoned and Mom didn't appreciate her grandmother's dishware being used in a murder plot, pretend or otherwise. She and Dad didn't speak for a week. I wonder if Mya remembers this, too, but if she does, she doesn't say anything.

Mom's unearthed the set from its box tonight, though, doing her best not to let the cups rattle between her trembling hands.

I think Dad must hear the *clink* of the teacups from the basement, or maybe he hears the men, but he ambles up the stairs for the first time in a week. He smells like he hasn't showered for at least three days and his five o'clock shadow is somewhere around eleven p.m. His argyle sweater and brown pants hang on his limbs like rags on a scarecrow, and if the tips of his mustache were any pointier, they might be able to prop up his sagging forehead.

As frightening as Dad looks, though, the two men in black suits scare me more.

There's nothing specifically eerie about them, except that they clearly aren't twins or even related but somehow still look like the same person. One is blond and fair with soft curves to his face; the other has an olive complexion and hard angles. Yet both have hair crisply parted to the right, black shoes reflecting our dim living room light, legs and backs straight. They look somehow rigid but also perfectly at home in our home.

I already can't wait for them to leave.

"First, we must apologize for dropping in on you unannounced," says the man with the dark hair and sharp jaw. I like to pretend his name is Bob. The other man, who I pretend is Dirk, remains standing, holding his teacup and saucer in front of his sternum.

"I suppose this is better than being followed around town," my mom says, and even though she chirps a little laugh, it's obvious that nothing about this is funny to her.

"Ah," says Bob, contrite but unsurprised. "A second apology is in order. We didn't mean to frighten you, but measures had to be taken, specific measures . . ."

"Accuracy," says Dirk from his place against the wall, lifting the teacup to his lips without moving any other part of his body.

Bob nods. "Accuracy."

None of this makes any sense to me.

Aside from the tiny sips the men in suits take, the room is completely quiet. Mya shifts from foot to foot, Dad has taken a seat and now sits hunched in what used to be his favorite armchair, and Mom is standing behind him, almost like she's guarding him, her hand pressed into his shoulder.

"This tea is lovely," Bob says. "Is that . . . citrus?"

Mom blinks at him.

"It is," she says. And then, "But you're not here about tea, I'm presuming."

Now *this* is the mom I know and love, the woman who could land a triple pirouette without flinching, the mom who made our family hum like a machine before Germany and everything afterward happened.

Bob clears his throat and slowly sets his teacup down on the coffee table. He doesn't look up. Instead, he looks at his hands, folded delicately in his lap.

"As you are likely aware, the Fernweh Welt incident is still under federal investigation," he says, wasting zero time in setting aside the niceties.

One look at Mom tells me she regrets this. I'm guessing she'd love to still be talking about citrus tea right now. I'm guessing we all would.

Except for Dad. Dad . . . almost looks better. Like he's lined up for a race he already knows he's going to lose, but he's just glad to finally be running it.

"I suspect you already knew that the investigation was ongoing, though, isn't that right, Mr. Peterson?" he says.

Dad says nothing.

"I suspect you knew that we wanted to speak to you before you, *ahem*, unceremoniously left Germany to move to this . . . town." He says "town" like it's a dirty word.

My dad shifts in his chair. Mom squeezes his shoulder hard enough to turn her knuckles white. Mya begins swaying closer toward me, and that's probably good because maybe if I lean toward her, we can prop each other up and not fall over. I'm pretty sure my legs are about to give out.

Finally, Dirk speaks, but it really doesn't matter who's doing the talking because they're both saying the same thing.

"We might have been tempted to rule the Fernweh Welt incident an accident if not for the impressive investigative journalism of your local television station," he says, and his words hang in the air for a moment, like laundry out to dry.

Channel Four. Even on the brink of bankruptcy, they're determined to make our lives miserable.

"How dare you insinuate that tragedy was anything but an accident," Mom says. "An accident we don't think about every day, an accident we don't hold in our hearts." Dad reaches up to hold the hand she's pressing into his shoulder.

"I have no doubt you think about it every day," says Bob.

"Or perhaps . . ." Dirk sets his cup and saucer on the side table and slowly moves away from the wall.

I'm pretty sure every muscle in my body goes rigid.

"Perhaps, there's more to these accidents. Perhaps there's something more . . . sinister at play."

To everyone's surprise, it's Mya who pipes in next.

"So how come you're here and not the police? The *real* police?" she says, and holy bagels, I think the men's smiles slip. For just that second, they look mad. All I can think is *Wow. My sister is a hero.*

I know I have to be her backup.

"Yeah," I say, clearing my throat. "Shouldn't a Raven Brooks detective be questioning us?"

I mean, nobody should be questioning us, but still.

The men exchange a look I don't like at all. They shuffle toward the door.

"Oh, you're so right, young man," Dirk says to me, his hand hovering by the door. "In fact, I do suspect you'll be hearing from the Raven Brooks authorities soon. I understand more than one tragedy has befallen this, ah, town. There's still that missing man to find, right?"

Dirk lets his question linger in the air as he reaches for the doorknob.

"I'm sure we'll be seeing each other quite soon," Bob says.

And then the two depart—two shadowy, confusing figures who get back into their awful black car.

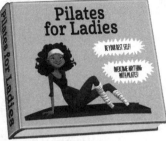

For a moment, we're all silent—Mom, Dad, Mya, and me. We wait with bated breath to hear the car's ignition turn on, then the car turn out of our driveway and be on its way. Once we can no longer hear the car, Mom leans her head against the big wooden door. I can hear her take long, deep breaths. I wonder if she learned these breaths from the *Pilates for Ladies* book, too. If I listened closer, I might even be able to hear her counting.

While Mom counts, I focus my attention on Dad. He runs a hand through his hair and then, quick as a flash, disappears back down to the basement.

Mom hears him creak on the third step and opens her eyes. She says one word.

My dad stops for a second.

"Work," he says, but it looks like he's talking to the hallway and not her.

"Ted."

Then he does look up at all of us, and if only he weren't standing in the dark shadows of the stairs, I might be able to see his eyes. I might be able to understand.

"I love you," he says.

Maybe he says it to Mom, or maybe he says it to all of us, I'm not sure. But it doesn't matter anyway. Will Dad loving us make the investigators go away? Will love keep my mom from needing to hold our family together while my dad saws away at it with a serrated knife? Would love have made Lucy Yi survive?

No sooner does the basement door shut than my mom grips the remote control, flipping wildly through the channels. I guess there's a lot of responses I could have expected, just not . . . that.

Mya's noticed, too.

"Mom?" Mya prompts.

"Gah!" Mom yells and throws the remote down onto the couch. "Call me when that lawyer commercial comes on," she says. "You shouldn't have to wait long. It played on repeat tirelessly last week when I was trying to watch the volleyball game."

Then she grumbles something about how anyone could pay money for a lawyer on a horse.

Mya and I exchange a look of utter horror. There's only one lawyer commercial we see play seemingly on loop on TV . . . and that's Jed Jed the Law Man.

A shiver comes up and down my spine. Jed Jed the Law Man is the stuff of Saturday-morning nightmares. His stupid commercials air every ten minutes, between every cartoon and action series, always with that stupid grin and riding some poor, sad horse that looks like there's nothing more it hates than being on television. Seriously, I'm surprised animal rights activists haven't stormed his corporate offices yet.

"Maybe we should try someone more . . . er, reputable?" I suggest.

Mom gives me a look I've never seen before. It actually kind of takes me aback.

"Don't you think I've tried?" she says.

It's just a sentence—a small, single statement—but it carries the burden that I realize we're *all* carrying. We're all trying our best. Me, Mom, Mya, maybe even Dad.

"Okay," I reply, because I'm not sure what else there is to say. I hear Mya sniffle just once.

Mom freezes.

"Oh . . . oh, kids. I'm sorry. I'm so sorry."

"No, no," I sputter. "It's okay."

She shakes her head. "I've . . . we've . . . done everything we can to keep you kids as far away from this," she says, crossing her arms over her chest. She looks so small all of a sudden.

"Mom, it's okay," I say, because I just want this conversation to be over.

"We'll call you when we see the commercial," Mya says, standing up straight, sounding way more adult than all of us.

There isn't anything else to discuss, so Mom nods her head and walks into the kitchen with the tray of fancy teacups. I wouldn't be surprised if I heard each little flowered saucer crash against a wall and become porcelain dust on the floor.

The TV is now playing the news on Channel Seven.

It's Gordon Cleave, squinting into the glare of a sudden spotlight. He looks like a mole seeing daylight for the first time in a month.

"Where is he, the sewer?" Mya says.

"Er," I say, but it only takes another second for me to see the familiar door of the basement to the Golden Apple Factory behind him.

"Mr. Cleave! Mr. Cleave!" a reporter yells into her microphone. "Can you comment on the restructuring of the Channel Four News organization?"

"Wh-what?" he stammers.

"The reorganization of your newsroom. We understand from the board of directors that your severance has been rescinded. Did you see it coming?"

"My severance has been . . . ?"

"No. Way," Mya says breathlessly.

"Mr. Cleave, you've had a long, storied career in the media. Will this mean early retirement for you?"

"Retirement?"

I didn't think it was possible to feel sorry for Gordon Cleave, but a little, icky splotch of sympathy spreads through me. Kind of like mold.

Then a sudden realization dawns on me.

"We've got to get to the tunnels."

"What? Why?" Mya quips.

I take a deep breath. "Whatever Cleave is doing in the tunnels . . . has gotta be what he was trying to do when I caught him down there on Opening Day."

Mya's face looks a little paler than usual. "But you barely got out of there with your life." She flinches at what she's just said.

"I was also close to finding out what he was doing," I say. "And whatever it is, I'm positive it has to do with us."

Finally, Mya seems to understand, but I can tell she doesn't like it.

"How do you suggest we get to the tunnels?" she says.

Right. Dad is in the basement. There's no way we can use it as an escape route to the tunnels—and no way we can think of another route to the tunnels.

I look back to the TV screen, trying to analyze it. Something, anything. There's gotta be a clue. After what feels like a million seconds of staring at the TV, I see it—poking out through the tiny left corner of the screen. It's the Factory door, still ajar from where it caught on the clump of overgrowth.

* * *

But we don't leave right away. As much as we want to. We can't.

The black sedan has moved from where it was parked earlier this afternoon, but only enough to prove that the German investigators don't intend to let us out of their sight. Sneaking out of the house and into the forest is near impossible with them squatting right there on the side of the street.

"That one guy had a pudding face," Mya says, her head against the wall.

"Huh?"

"His face, it was like dough. Like you could mush it around, and all the features would go back to their places but, like, really slowly. Like it was moving through pudding."

I nod. She's not wrong.

But I'm trying not to think of the investigators' faces. I'm trying to think about the geometry I'm terrible at.

"If we move at a sixty-degree angle from the base of the tree to the hedge across the street, I think we might have enough coverage from the trestle to climb over the fence and access the path to the forest from their backyard," I say out loud.

She shakes her head. "I don't know. That's cutting it pretty close. I mean, if they see us, the only choice we'll have is to head for the porch of that turquoise house, and then what? We'll be cornered."

We're in my room now. But the longer we stare out the window from my bedroom, the more it looks as though my idea isn't just the best one—it's the *only* one. No matter what, we have to get across the street.

Against Mya's better judgment—and honestly, mine too—we head out.

I'm the first to shimmy down the tree. Then I signal to Mya to take her turn.

Once we're both on the ground, we crouch as low as possible.

"We should go at the same time," she says. "Less chance of them detecting movement."

I nod. "We make a beeline for the hedge, then back up against the trestle."

"And if we get caught?" she says.

I think. "Then we're dead," I say.

Mya thinks about this for a moment. "All right. On three."

We crouch lower.

"One."

Mya takes a step sideways.

"Two."

We watch the black sedan and pull in a deep breath.

"Three!"

It turns out my geometry isn't just bad. It's terrible.

We're three-quarters of the way across the street when the black car's headlights switch on, casting a spotlight inches from the back of my heel.

It isn't even a conversation. We flee for the one place we both agreed was the worst place to be cornered—the dead end that is the porch belonging to the empty turquoise house.

"We're dead, we're dead, we're very, very, very dead," Mya whispers into my shoulder as we crouch behind the hedge. Her breath beads through my shirt.

"Shh," I hiss.

In the midnight quiet of Friendly Court, I hear the unmistakable click of a car door opening. A second later, the slow crunch of a foot presses against the asphalt once, then twice, then a third time.

The footsteps move in time, almost like they're set to a clock, ensuring perfect cadence.

And they're ticking closer with every step.

Mya's eyes widen in the dark of the porch, and I pull her shoulder tighter toward me. She buries her head in my armpit.

There's no place to go, and these footsteps aren't backing away.

I look around frantically, but the darkened porch offers little more than an untended hedge and a pot full of dead flowers by the door.

Except hadn't there been a lockbox on that door at some point?

Another step closer, and I move the tiniest bit, which makes Mya dig her fingers into my arm.

I bite my tongue to keep from crying out in pain and instead grasp her chin in my other hand and turn her head toward the door.

She looks back at me and shakes her head in fast flicks.

I nod just as quickly, though, and three more steps will bring those feet around the corner.

One thing is for certain: If we don't move, we're caught for sure. If we do move, we have a teeny, tiny chance of getting into that house and ducking out of sight.

From my crouch, I lift my hand to the knob and turn. I nearly faint when the door falls open, miraculously without a sound.

Mya scoots in after me, and I ease the door shut just as the foot rounds the corner.

Once our backs are against the door, we hold a collective breath and strain our ears to hear. The footsteps have stopped.

I turn to Mya. Her eyes are squeezed shut. I can't even manage to blink.

Nobody knows we're here.

I tell myself to shut up, but I never listen. My thoughts are running wild.

Nobody knows we're here, and the investigators could open this door and stuff us into their car and drive off and no one would see or hear from us ever again. Dad will be arrested and Mom will have to hire Jed Jed the Law Man. The worst part, though, is that we'll never be found. Maybe because no one will even look for us . . .

Then the footsteps recede.

One step, then the next, then another.

They travel down the driveway. They reach the gravelly asphalt.

The door of a car thuds shut, its finality echoing across the street and through the door we lean against.

Beside my foot lies an empty can of rust remover, seemingly bragging about the wonderful job it did on the old hinges of the front door.

I've never wanted to kiss a bottle of grease until now.

Mya gets up and seems to regain her wits faster than I do.

"They must be getting ready to rent this place out," she says, eyeing the fresh paint around the trim of the door.

I shrug. "Lucky us, I guess."

Mya scrunches up her nose as we pass the worn stairs and move into the shabby kitchen.

"Can't say the same for whoever gets to live in this dump," she says.

"It's not like we live in a palace," I say, but even I know that our house is better than this one. Sometimes, a house is lived in too many times. Each time someone moves out, their memories get painted over, until it doesn't feel like a house at all.

Mya eases the sliding glass door open to the backyard. It doesn't take us long to find a loose fence post in the overgrown garden. I hear my heart thump loud in my chest. I can't believe we did it.

We pick our way through the now-familiar overgrowth, ducking and weaving through the various attempts at barricading all entrances.

"I don't see why someone hasn't just mowed this entire forest down," Mya says.

"That seems a little extreme."

"Is it? How many awful things have happened here? I mean, between the whole Forest Protector fake-out, the Factory fire, Mr. Gershowitz going missing . . . all anyone ever does is put up some NO TRESPASSING signs and yellow tape. Do they really think that's going to keep people out?"

The more I think about what Mya's saying, the more I shudder. The only thing worse than a cursed forest where no one is welcome is a cursed forest where ALL are welcome.

I'm so engrossed in Mya's horrifying theory that I don't realize we've unconsciously taken the path that brings us right past the entrance of the Golden Apple Amusement Park.

ALL ARE WELCOME! COME ON IN. THE FOREST ISN'T CREEPY AT ALL.

"It looks different in the dark," I say, staring up at the entrance archway.

It seems like a hundred years ago that the people of Raven Brooks were shuffling anxiously through the line to the ticket booth, ready for a day of family fun and Golden Apples.

It's not the dark that makes the park look so different now, though. It's that I know. I know what tragedy has befallen here. And it's almost like I can hear Lucy's voice, echoing . . . her scream . . .

Mya's looking right at me. If I didn't know better, I'd think she actually heard Lucy's scream, too.

"I have to see it," she says.

"What?"

Mya looks at the ground.

"Where it—where it happened," she stammers.

"Mya—"

"You weren't there," Mya cuts in.

I can't argue with that logic.

"Okay," I say. "Okay."

We walk through the park, me and Mya. The rest of the park is so intact, so pristine, it's almost grotesque. It's like the park is mocking us—laughing at the accident. If you didn't know better, you might think nothing horrible ever even happened here. But there are hints if you know where to look.

There are the flies beginning to take over the vending stand that still hasn't been cleared of its sticky Golden Apples. There are the plush toys that have slowly begun to be pulled apart by the resident crows, their sharp beaks picking away at the seams. There are crumpled game tickets and abandoned wristbands that have migrated to the corners of the walkways. The colors of the park are muted and gray under the midnight sky.

Mya reaches the Rotten Core first.

"How could we have been so stupid?" she says, and her voice sounds rough and wrong for her.

I don't know what to say. I wonder if there's anything we could have done. I wonder if maybe everyone's right. If Lucy's blood *is* on our hands, because we didn't stop our dad. But that can't be true . . . right?

Mya makes a noise that sounds like a tiny, frightened cry.

When I look at her, though, I realize she isn't crying. No, she's trying not to *scream*.

The hair on my arms rises, and I want so badly to help her, scoop her up like when she was little and tell her everything would be okay. But then I realize that Mya isn't trying not to scream because of Lucy.

She's trying not to scream because something is in the bushes.

CHAPTER 4

Mya takes off like a rocket. I follow her.

We dash through the park, straight for the Rotten Core and to the back. But neither of us knows where that way leads—or even if there's a path. The whole idea of sneaking through the forest was to avoid detection getting into the tunnels; whoever is barreling toward us isn't stopping to think. They're not stopping at all.

I take the lead this time and break through the tree line in the only direction I know to travel—toward the Weather Station and the Factory.

"Are they still behind us?" I call over my shoulder.

"I can't tell."

I can practically feel the fear radiating off Mya. Or maybe that's my fear. Whoever's terror it is, hopefully it'll propel us a little bit faster. I hear the rattle of branches and the snaps of twigs, and it sounds like whatever was in the bushes is steps away from us.

"They're gaining," Mya huffs, and I know she's right, but I can barely see where I'm going between the dark and the overgrowth. Branches and vines jut and drape across our path, making every step a chance for peril.

Mya guides me through the fork in the path that leads to the Factory door.

We slow down just enough to notice that the door to the basement is still partially open, probably from when Gordon Cleave exited on TV.

We race to the door and, once safely inside, pull it shut. The door clangs loudly, making us both wince against the noise.

I lock the door but refuse to let go of the handle, because whoever might be on the other side could have a key. Mya presses her ear against the metal. Both of our heartbeats are beating fast—did all that really just happen?

After what feels like two whole breaths, I hear the sound of leaves crunching outside, and I don't need to read Mya's face to know that the same fear etched on mine is emblazoned on hers. The crunching grows closer, one step at a time, closing the space between us and them.

When the footsteps finally stop, I feel a pressure on the door, as though someone is leaning against it on the other side. They're listening—listening for *us*.

Mya reaches up and squeezes my wrist. I hold my breath until it feels like my lungs might pop and splatter all over this door.

Then, in my hand, I feel the slow turn of a knob trying to budge against its lock. I try to keep it shut tight, but the handle persists, turning against my grip.

What if I can't hang on?

My palm is on fire, and the muscles in my arms quake, but if I stop now, we're done for.

Then—slowly—the tension on the handle begins to release. Whoever is on the other side backs away.

We wait until we can't hear the footsteps anymore. Then we wait even longer. When I finally do let go of the door handle, it's only because the muscles in my hands finally give out.

"The German detectives," Mya says, and it's somehow both a question and a statement. "Do you think it's safe to turn on a light?"

I nod. "There aren't any windows down here. I don't see why not."

I hear a tinny clink from Mya, and a second later, a dim yellow light flickers from a caged light bulb on the ceiling. The strobing of the light is making my eyes hurt, but bad light is better than no light, I suppose.

At least that's what I think until I look around at the vacant Golden Apple Factory basement and see what it's become.

Everywhere I turn, black-and-gray fingerprints smudge every surface in the entire basement. Little numbered sticky notes are tacked to many of the smudges—even the door we barreled through.

"What . . . happened here?" Mya gasps. I've got to be honest. I'm thinking the same thing.

Not far from the door handle, I see a pink piece of paper taped up against the door. It's got some print on it. I lean forward, eager to see what it says.

I read the notice three times before I realize what it actually means.

"Aaron, we *really* shouldn't be here," Mya says.

"Would you rather be out *there*?" I say, gesturing to whatever awaits us on the other side.

She doesn't answer me. Instead, she moves slowly around the room, touching each of the smudges like she's trying to match her own fingerprints to them.

Meanwhile, I walk around and discover a low hutch of a desk that's holding various binders stuffed with paper.

Discarded on the desk is another notice with the Raven Brooks Police Department seal, only this one screams in bold letters: WARRANT. I look closer.

I stare at the slip of paper, mouth agape. My mind can't get over the word. The big *M* word. *Murder.* Then—*Ike Quentin Cornelius Gershowitz.* This isn't real. None of this can be real.

Mya must sense my stupor because she comes over to see what's wrong. She reads the notice in the crack between my arm and the desk.

"They think Mr. Gershowitz is . . ." Mya starts, but we both know she doesn't need to finish. *We* knew Mr. Gershowitz might be dead. *We* knew it

By order of the District Court of the town of Raven Brooks, the Court does hereby authorize representatives of the Raven Brooks Police Department to search the premises of the property **"Golden Apple Factory"** – ownership ascribed to Tillman Partners, LLC – for evidence of the following suspected crime(s):

- Murder
- Conspiracy to commit murder
- Conspiracy to obstruct an investigation

This WARRANT permits the Raven Brooks Police Department to collect evidence about or relating to the above suspected crimes pertaining to the suspected murder of the following victim(s):
- Ike Quentin Cornelius Gershowitz

As approved and signed by the Honorable Justice Horatio M. Perez-Gutierrez the longer he was gone. *We* knew it when his wallet—his *bloody* wallet—went missing.

What we didn't know was that the Raven Brooks Police thought he was dead, too.

"Why would they be searching the basement of the Golden Apple Factory for evidence of . . . this?" I say, pointing to the warrant.

"I don't know," Mya says, "but we have to leave."

I can't argue with that.

I'm just about to follow Mya to the door that leads to the tunnels when another fluttering paper catches my eye.

A folded copy of the *Raven Brooks Banner* sits patiently on a chair beside the desk, as though waiting to be discovered. And I don't know why this takes me by surprise, but it's opened—where else—to the crossword page.

"Hang on," I tell Mya.

I squint through the blinking light at the puzzle. It's a newer issue, one I haven't seen yet. Maybe because this is the third time I've found a copy of the paper turned to the puzzles page, but I get the strangest feeling that I'm *supposed* to be stumbling on them.

"I need a pen," I say.

"Now? You want to play games right *now*?" Mya says. For a moment, I can hear a bit of my mom's voice, almost like she's talking to our dad. I never thought they sounded similar before, so it catches me off guard.

I scan the area and find an old, moldy pencil underneath the desk. Then I look at the crossword puzzle in front of me.

"I've got a hunch," I say. "One second."

Mya shifts uneasily. "Would you just hurry?"

I'll hurry as fast as I can, I think. Then I read the first clue aloud. *"Seen best through the looking glass, or so Alice found."*

I do a quick count of the spaces allotted in the crossword. Eleven. A companion of Alice—looking glass—I test my first guess.

CATERPILLAR

It fits. I move on to the next one.

"The tiniest dot made this Starry Night . . ."

"Starry Night, like the painting?" Mya says.

"Yeah," I reply.

I count eleven squares and fill in POINTILLISM. Thank you, Mrs. Ryland, for randomly going on a tangent about art techniques while teaching us about French geography.

I move on to the third clue. *"The Queen of Fruits, this legendary food once fetched a reward of one hundred sterling pounds from Queen Victoria . . .* What in the world—?"

"MANGOSTEEN," Mya interjects.

It fits.

"How could you possibly know that?" I say.

Mya shrugs. "You know art, I know fruit."

We move through the puzzle together, gritting our teeth as it gets harder, but determined to finish before leaving. Mya's hooked now, and I hope my suspicion is right. Any moment the police can break in and we're doomed.

Once we've filled in the last answer, I rotate the paper round and round until, finally, I can see something resembling a message.

restore the balance

Mya slumps. "*That's* what we spent all this time on? 'Restore the balance'?"

"It has to mean something," I insist.

But with the minutes ticking by, there's one thing I know Mya's right about. We need to get moving if we're going to make it back home without detection.

"Observatory or Weather Station?" Mya says pointedly.

"Mya, if you think I have a plan, you don't know me at all."

Mya laughs. I think she was just looking for directions, and I don't blame her. Sometimes you need a direction to move forward. It's one of those rare moments that I wish I was a younger sibling, just to be under someone's wing. Not that Mya is ever really under my wing, but hopefully you know what I mean.

I take the lead anyway, knowing both the Observatory and the Weather Station are at least in the same direction. Maybe we'll find some clue along the way of what Mr. Cleave was up to before the *News Seven* cameras caught him—if we're lucky.

We move through my chosen path in silence, each of our hearts pounding to our own thoughts. I'm guessing that Mya and I are in a similar place. We just want answers, we want to not be caught, we're hoping beyond hope that Mom and Dad haven't noticed we're missing.

"At least we know it wasn't a Forest Protector chasing us," Mya says after we've traveled a few minutes.

"Is that supposed to be a silver lining?"

I actually do have another theory, one I've been trying to decide whether or not to bring up. But now's as good a time as any.

"It could have been Dad," I say.

Silence follows. I can tell that thought occurred to Mya, too.

"Dad wouldn't," Mya says in a small voice, and for a moment I agree—I think, of course not. Of course not. Most definitely . . . almost definitely not. Dad wouldn't . . .

"Not *after* us," I say, softening the blow. "Maybe more like . . . just trying to scare us away."

"Okay," Mya concedes, "so then we're back to, why would Dad try to stop us from finding out the truth? If all we're doing is trying to find something that will prove he's innocent . . . there should be nothing to hide, right?"

I don't want to answer her. I don't think she even needs me to. We both know, as we found out a few months ago, that Dad took Mr. Gershowitz's wallet from me in the hospital when I fell out of a tree. We both know he practically banned us from saying the name Gershowitz in his presence. And we both know, deep down, it has something mysterious to do with our grandparents and their weather station.

And now Dad's being investigated for the accident at Fernweh Welt—the flume ride.

I'm running out of excuses for him, if I'm being honest.

"Can we just go back to believing in the Forest Protectors?"

Mya says, and I think she's only half joking. "I mean, it's still pretty freaky." She lowers her voice. "A bunch of grown-ups dressing like birds, meeting in some weird observatory for a bonkers light show and doohickeys that are somehow worth breaking and entering for?"

"That settles it, then," I say. "We'll hit the Observatory first. If we're lucky, maybe we can find whatever Gordon Cleave was up to."

In a way, it's good that we have a plan. In another sense, we're not sure if this is the right one.

We aren't even that close to the Observatory when we start hearing echoes of voices. I strain my ears.

"I'm telling you, it's not going to work without Cleave!"

Mya and I barely look at each other before speeding ahead on tiptoe, inching as fast as we can toward the Observatory. After I basically destroyed the entrance the last time I was here, we can't risk getting too close, so once we see light, we dart to the side, backing against the wall and leaning as close as we can to hear more.

"Forget about Cleave. There's nothing we can do for him now."

"Idiot dug his own grave."

"Careful. It could happen to any of us. One little slipup and the fortune shifts. We all know the rules."

All the voices sound vaguely familiar, but I can't seem to put a name to any of them. It's like they're hanging out in the back of my brain, some remnant from memories I've long forgotten.

"Yeah, if you call that a slipup. More like sabotage."

"C'mon, you really think a bunch of kids are capable of a plot like that?"

Ice rushes through my veins as I turn to Mya, whose trembling hands tell me she heard it, too.

A bunch of kids.

"Yeah, as a matter of fact I do. And if you *don't* think so, then you're a fool. The main kid's a Peterson, and you know as well as I do what kind of trouble a Peterson can make. The little girl's just a follower, but that boy, he's an instigator."

"Follower?" Mya hisses. *"Little girl?"* I clap my hand over her mouth before she can make too much noise.

"But we know how to take care of that trouble, too."

It seems I've forgotten how to move.

The room rumbles with a low laughter that reminds me of thunder. I feel numb. If we don't get taken down by any number of horrifying adults by the end of the night, I'm pretty sure a heart attack will do me in.

By the time a little feeling does return to my hand, it's only because Mya is tugging on it. *We have to GO*, she mouths.

I don't argue. What I *do* is take a step. The wrong step. A very loud step. Yeesh.

Rubble from the previous opening of the door rolls under my foot, sending a small chunk of rock skittering through the echoing tunnels.

The rumble of laughter in the Observatory screeches to a halt.

"I heard it, too. That came from the tunnels," someone says.

"Go," Mya hisses at me and disappears around the corner toward the passage leading to our basement.

Suddenly, the passages seem darker than they've ever been.

"Mya," I whisper, not daring to call out any louder. Behind me, I hear the scamper of grown people climbing and stumbling through the opening at the top of the Observatory. The voices swirl around us.

"Did you hear them?"

"Which way did they go?"

"I can't risk being seen here!"

"None of us can risk that, Tapps!"

"Don't use my name!"

I press on, making my feet as light as possible on the tunnel floors. I try desperately to remember which sections had the biggest divots for puddles to collect. Even the tiniest splash could give my location away.

But with all the sound bouncing around from the Observatory, I can't tell backward from forward. I'm moving purely on instinct at this point, trusting my feet can remember the twists and turns of the passages back home.

That's an awful lot of trust to put in my feet, which I realize pretty fast when I run headfirst into the corner of a wall.

Right or left? Right or left?

I can't remember, and where is Mya, and did one of them say "Tapps"? As in Detective Dale Tapps?

Then, in the space of two quick breaths, a set of footsteps approaches, fumbling through the dark right toward me.

"Come out, come out, wherever you are," a singsongy voice calls through the tunnels, voice tickling my ear.

"I'm not gonna hurt you," the voice says. And if there's

anything more horrifying than the sound of a winded grown-up lying, it's a *scared*, winded grown-up lying.

I risk a step to my right, but I immediately realize that's a huge mistake. The man moves in the same direction, placing himself so close to me, I can actually smell the garlic on his breath from whatever he ate last. It hits me in a big wave, and I make a mental note of it. Garlic.

He can hear my heart beating. He can hear my blood pumping. Don't move. Don't move. Do. Not. Move.

I think I'm done for. As I'm thinking what must be my final thoughts (of all things, I'm thinking about the piece of lettuce Mom had in her teeth last week), a fleet of footsteps comes hurtling through the tunnels, and the man with the garlic breath whips around, hitting me in the face with a feathery cloak. Less than a foot away from where I stand, there's a crack, then a thud, then a curse, then a rumple of more cloaks and more feathers.

"Now I've got you!" calls a voice.

"Get off of me, you maniac!"

"Tapps?"

"If you use my name one more time, Harold, I swear—"

"Shhh! Are you out of your mind?"

"Get off of me!"

"Quiet, you two! Do you want to bring us all down? C'mon, it's over."

"But—"

"Leave it! We don't even know if there was anyone there!"

"There was—"

"I said *let's go!*"

The man with the garlic breath pants once or twice more, and I brace myself for his final attempt. I picture him lunging straight for the wall I'm hoping will absorb me. But Detective Dale rustles some more, and I think he's on his feet, and I think the garlic man has turned, walking away. Could it be? It is.

I think they're leaving.

I don't let myself believe they're gone until I hear the very last footstep disappear into the tunnels, someplace too far to reach me.

To reach *us*.

Mya.

I cobble together what's left of my courage and peel myself from the wall, feeling around until I find the corner I met with my head moments before.

"Mya, where are you?"

I whisper at first, then say it a little louder. "Mya? Come on!"

But the only answer I get is the echo of my own terrified voice.

I've lost her. Again.

What if one of the others got to her? What if they're dragging her away, through the dark tunnels while she waits for me to save her?

But no, she was ahead of me. There's no way they could have gotten to her. There's no way. There's no way.

"There's no way."

I say it again and again. I say it with each step I take through the last remaining tunnel before the turn that takes me back to the basement, back to safety.

"There's no way. She's safe. She's safe. She made it out and she's safe."

I burst through the basement door and into Dad's office. I didn't realize until pushing the passage door open that I'd been holding out hope that Mya would be there waiting for me, waiting to scold me for falling so far behind.

Waiting to scold me for scaring her to death.

Thankfully, Dad isn't there. The only sound I hear upon entering is my own sobbing—sobbing I didn't even know I was doing.

It's a fraction of a second before I look up and skid to a stop in the downstairs hallway. There before me is Mya, her eyes as round as the moon in the sky.

"Mya!" I gasp, not sure whether I want to squeeze her or shake her. "Where did you—?"

Before I can finish my sentence, I notice that Mya has barely moved. I don't even think she's blinked.

"Mya . . . ?"

Then I see it. There's a hand grasping Mya's shoulder.

It's Dad.

CHAPTER 5

"**D**ad, I can explain—" I begin.

Dad silences me with a mere look.

"Go upstairs," he says to us both.

I don't understand. Where's the inquisition? The outrage? Where's that whispering thing he does when he's so mad he thinks whispering makes it better but it actually makes it a hundred times worse?

We stand there, two dummies waiting to be wound up.

"Now," he says sharply, and this time, there's no waiting.

Mya and I tackle the stairs two at a time, practically climbing over one another in our race to the top.

Just before we reach the landing, Dad says in a voice so small I have to repeat it in my head a dozen times to be sure I heard it, "If I hear either of your doorknobs so much as turn, you'll never see daylight again."

He means it. He means every word. We flee before he can apply any more conditions on our already miraculous clemency.

"He didn't even—" I start to say.

"Shhh," Mya replies. "Later."

I nod. We close ourselves in our respective rooms, grateful they aren't tombs.

As soon as I get my body to stop shaking, I sneak to my window and look for the black sedan. But all I find is an empty, moon-soaked street. Curious.

No matter how relieved I am that Mya and I weren't caught in the forest, we still don't know who was chasing us.

And what's more, we still don't know what they were doing there *or* what they were so desperate to keep secret.

I know that Mya and I were lucky Dad only banished us to our rooms and didn't subject us to the interrogation he normally would have. But it's all rather suspicious. Any parent would want to know where their kids were sneaking out to. Right?

This is what life has come to—worrying about the things that *don't* get me into trouble.

I worry until the moonlight trades places with sunlight and breakfast appears on a tray outside each of our rooms. But the trays are just another reminder of the strange events of the evening. Nevertheless, I'm hungry, and the veggie sausage smells great.

All of this only makes me want to talk to Mya more.

I scribble a note down and open my door one muffled creak at a time. It wouldn't surprise me if Dad had mounted motion-detecting cameras in the hallway to catch any evidence of our delinquency. But the hallway is clear, at least as far as I can tell.

The note I have is simple, just enough to get Mya to come back with a single answer. It says:

Where were you?

I slide the paper under her door and creep back into my room.

After what feels like an eternity, I feel the floor under my feet bow the tiniest bit. I wait for her response to slide under the crack, and sure enough, there's the corner peeking through, caught on the carpet. I snatch it up quickly.

Where were <u>you</u>?? I fainted!! Well, I think I fainted. I've never actually fainted before, so I wouldn't know what it feels like. It was so weird! Anyway, I fell, and I think I was sliding down a long slide-type thing or whatever. Or maybe that was part of a dream. Wait, do you dream when you faint?

This has to be the most infuriating note I've ever read. I've been waiting all night for *this*?

I grab my marker and try again.

How did you faint? Before or after you fell? What do you mean a slide? Details, Mya!!

I crack the door again. But then I hear a clatter coming from the kitchen, which makes me shrink back. I used to have a pet hermit crab named Max that refused to come out of its shell if it detected even the slightest threat, and I think I've never related more to that crab in my life.

After listening through the door for another minute, I take the few steps needed to reach Mya's door and shove the paper under, then dart back to my room.

Another agonizing wait. Finally, I hear a door ease open.

The paper that Mya slips under is new. She must have run out of room. This one is pink and framed in grapevines; it looks like she got it from the school book fair. Mya's written in three different colors.

> **Grumper.**
>
> **I don't know if I fainted. I told you, I've never done it before. I think it was after I fell, though. I remember falling, then sliding, then that's it. Until I was, like, floating. And then—Dad. What's up with Dad?**
>
> **Okay, but here's something even freakier. Even though I was probably dreaming, I felt like I was in our house. Like, that whole time, after I fell, it seemed like I was in our house. You know how it always smells kind of like Mom's burnt spaghetti sauce in here? That's what my dream smelled like.**

I don't know where to go with that one. How could she have slid a long enough distance to clunk her head, possibly knock herself semi-unconscious, and *still* wind up in our house?

> **Exactly how hard did you hit your head? Anyway, you heard Detective Dale in the tunnels, right? Could you make out any of their voices? And they were talking about us. Mya, they know about us!!!**

Mya's feet pad back.

> **DUH, they know about us. You made sure of that when you caught Cleave in the Observatory. Wait. Aaron, do you think they had anything to do with Mr. Gershowitz? Do they know the Golden Apple Factory basement was searched?**

How did I not even consider that? This means that the people who chased us in the tunnels might be the answer to proving Dad's innocence!

> **Then why doesn't Dad go after them? What's he waiting for?**

Mya slides the note back.

> **Maybe he doesn't know about them?**

I scratch my answer fast.

> **Do you believe that?**

I've just slid the note back under Mya's door when I hear the phone ring downstairs.

"Well, he's grounded," I hear Mom say. She waits for whoever is on the other line to answer and then responds, "I don't know why. Clearly, I just occupy space here now."

She pauses.

"A job?"

Another pause.

"I guess if he made a commitment . . . just make sure he comes right home *right* afterward. No stopping for hamburgers, nothing."

Mom's fast to move up the stairs, faster than I'm ready for, and I've nearly got my door closed when she slaps her palm against it.

"I just learned that you're the new crosswords editor at the *Raven Brooks Banner*," she spits, sounding annoyed when she says it.

"Oh yeah, I kinda forgot to mention that," I manage.

"You're a little young for a job," she says.

"It's more of a volunteer thing," I reply. "Enzo's doing it, too."

Mention of Enzo seems to lend my story the right amount of credibility.

"Well, you've made a commitment, and Petersons honor their commitments. Now get out. You're going to be late," she says.

I don't mean to be ungrateful. It's not that I'm thrilled at the prospect of staying locked in my room all day, but Mya and I have only scratched the surface of last night's weirdness. The last thing I feel like doing is pretending to care about a stupid newspaper crossword puzzle.

"I . . . uh . . . shouldn't I, like, see my punishment out? You know, take responsibility for my actions?"

Mom squints her eyes at me with renewed suspicion.

"If your father wants to enforce his prison sentence, he can come out of the basement and do it himself," she snips back.

Yikes. Marital problems, I guess? Maybe I *am* better off getting out of the house. I'm not sure I want to stick around to witness what happens on the off chance Dad does actually make an appearance.

* * *

When I walk through the doors of the *Banner*, I wonder for a minute if I'm in the right place. Sure, it's the *Banner*, but it's not the one I remember the few times I visited with Enzo. This bustling office—with cubicles crammed with people and files, tangles of phone cords and shouts from across the room for "copy" and "fact-checker" and "proof"—is not the same sleepy office that previously only needed one receptionist to manage a handful of phone lines.

Now the circular reception desk is staffed with three harried receptionists, handing messages backward to impatient reporters, transferring tip after tip to the editorial desk.

I'm dizzy just standing here watching the spectacle.

"Hey, Rudy, tell that proofreader I need him as soon as he's done with your feature!"

"Darlene, how are we coming on those classifieds?"

"I need a second source for the red panda story! Who's got a second source?"

It's another five minutes before one of the receptionists notices me.

"Who're you here for, punkin'?" she says, and I can smell the minty gum that's sandwiched between her teeth.

"Punkin'?"

"Speak up, sweets. It's louder than a boxing match in here."

"Um. I'm the new . . . er, I think I'm here for the puzzles?"

"The guzzles?"

"Puzzles. Like the crossword?" I manage.

She reaches for a button I can't see.

"Junior, come get ya friend!" she hollers into what I'm guessing is a speaker.

Just then, Enzo comes loping toward me from a narrow hallway to the left.

"Junior?"

Enzo shrugs. "I think they call me that because Dad works here. I dunno, it stuck."

I guess if you have to have one reputation from your dad, this isn't a bad one. I'm certainly not one to talk. I follow Enzo down the hallway he emerged from and the din of the front office fades enough to actually hear him.

Except he isn't saying anything. He didn't even look all that thrilled to see me.

Finally, when we reach an elevator, he talks.

"Guess you forgot?"

"Uh . . ."

"About your promise to work here?"

His tone is impossible to read. He's either annoyed that I forgot, annoyed that I'm here at all, or . . . maybe hurt.

"Yeah, um . . . I'm really sorry about that, Enzo," I say. It dawns on me that while I'd normally tell Enzo about my excursion last night, he doesn't want to hear it now. And maybe I don't even want to tell him. "I guess I just got distracted."

"Happens to you a lot lately, huh?" he says, but not like he's expecting an answer. More like it's just something he's been meaning to say to me for a while now.

A hot wave of guilt rushes through me.

"I'm sorry," I say sheepishly.

The elevator arrives with a weak ding, and to my disappointment, it's empty. Which means we get to enjoy this uncomfortable moment for a little bit longer. I feel like I need to fill the silence. Either that, or the elevator music is going to get us.

"Seriously, Enzo, I'm sorry," I repeat.

Enzo drops his head like I'm missing the whole point. Which I probably am. But it's not like he's making it easy for me to figure out, either. I can't shake the feeling that he's looking for a reason to be mad at me—like maybe that would be easier than admitting he thinks there's something wrong with me, or with my whole family.

"Anyway, I'll show you the office," he says as we arrive on the third floor and traverse another narrow hallway.

"Hey," I say, trying to lighten the mood, "remind you of anyplace?"

He stops mid-stride so fast, I almost bump into him.

"What?"

"You know," I say, chuckling even though none of this is really funny. "Narrow corridors and all . . . kind of like the tunnels, right?"

He furrows his bushy eyebrows and looks at me like . . . see, there it is again. The uncertainty. He's either worried about me or . . . this is what it looks like when someone is starting to hate you.

"Dude, not here. C'mon."

I take a deep breath and make myself push it out. Maybe just so I don't collapse into a deflated rubber version right here on the *Banner* carpet. Whatever Enzo is holding against me, it's not going away anytime soon.

"I know, you're right. It's just . . ." I start to say.

Enzo puts his palm close enough to my face for me to smell the lavender soap from the last time he washed his hands.

"I don't want to know."

"But—"

"Seriously, Aaron, I don't want to know. All this stuff . . . after Lucy, I just . . ."

Finally, I'm starting to see a shadow of the old Enzo, the guy who cared about more than the stupid newspaper or his crush on Trinity or which level of *BattleAxe 5000* he'd reached. He looks like he's aged ten years in the past ten days.

I look down at the floor. There's no trace of me down there, so he hasn't completely punctured me. But we're dangerously close to full deflation.

"Enzo, you know I didn't have anything to do with that, right?" I say. I can't figure out where I got the courage to blurt that out, but wherever it came from, it's too late to stuff back inside me now.

Enzo finds my eyes, and most of me believes the sincerity in them.

"I know that."

I guess that's why I go for it all.

"None of us did. Not even my dad."

I was so close. I was so incredibly close to finding my happy place with Enzo again. He was there. He was within reaching distance.

Until I mentioned my dad.

"I know," he says.

And I've never known anything with more certainty than I do in this moment—Enzo is lying to me.

Our "office" is at the end of the hall around a tight corner, and for good reason. The only thing that makes this an office and not the maintenance closet it was meant to be is the plate that's been pried from the outside of the door. Where I'm certain it once said CUSTODIAL or something like that, it now says JR. FEATURES—ENZO ESPOSITO (I guess that's really where "Junior" came from) and then, scribbled just below the already-crowded sign: AND PUZZLES.

I can't help but notice my name has been omitted. Enzo notices me noticing.

"I ran out of room," he says, which I'm sure

he thinks is easier to believe than "I didn't want my name next to 'Peterson.'"

"It's cool," I say, reminding myself that I didn't even want this job in the first place.

"Here," Enzo says, squeezing between the wall and one end of the desk that takes up the entire room. "I cleared you a space."

To Enzo's credit, he's given me half the desk, which obviously crowds his already limited work surface.

"Thanks," I say. "You know, I could do a lot of this out in the hallway or something. It's a little cramped."

"Whatever, let's just try not to get in each other's way," Enzo replies, which would sound perfectly harmless coming from a friend, but from post-accident Enzo, this barbed comment stings something awful.

I take my supplies—essentially blank proof paper, a pencil, a ruler, and the clues and answers provided by the Puzzle Master— and head for the hallway, where I will work on the floor.

It's a little ridiculous the amount of security that's been applied to the Puzzle Master materials. The envelope is marked CONFIDENTIAL on every available space, and it comes with strict instructions on who should open it (me and only me). There's also explicit directions on what should be done with the contents after the puzzle is designed (shred immediately). The envelope is stamped with an intricate filigree that appears specifically designed to cross over the seam of the envelope and to ensure that if the seal is broken, I would be able to tell.

I want to laugh with Enzo about the ridiculousness of this new Puzzle Master. It's not like this is a secret mission (although how awesome would that be if it *were*?). But, seriously. There isn't even a reward for completing the puzzle correctly like some newspapers offer.

When I peek back into the office, Enzo is hard at work, crossing out text and replacing it, tongue poking out of his mouth like it does when he's working super hard, which I guess he is.

He senses me staring at him.

"What?" he says, looking up for a second.

"Nothing," I reply.

Whatever that feeling in my stomach is, it's definitely not loneliness or isolation or embarrassment or woundedness or anger or bitterness or loneliness (which, yes, I already said, I realize that). This feeling isn't any of that. It's something . . . I can't describe.

I break the seal on the envelope with as much ceremony as I suspect the Puzzle Master would like me to use.

It occurs to me that this is the first time I'll get a look at the cryptic clues and their answers all at once, and I'm surprised to feel like maybe this *is* a little bit of a secret mission. Silly or not, I'm the only one who knows the answers to this puzzle at the moment. For the first time in as long as I can remember, I'm on the other side of the answers.

There are fifteen clues and corresponding answers, which might not seem like a lot, but there are only so many ways I can twist and turn the angles of the grid's rows and columns before I'm taking up more than my allotted space on the page.

Luckily my artistic eye really is an asset in this case. I'm still not at all convinced this is why the Puzzle Master asked for me specifically, but once I get into a groove, I sort of like the challenge of masking the answers in the perfect number of squares.

It takes me less time than I think it's going to. I can still hear Enzo scratching away in our office, so rather than make my thousandth attempt at talking to him the way we used to, I busy myself with reading through the clues. Up to this point, I'd been focusing mostly on the answers since those were what would dictate the grid. As single words or two-word terms, the answers were nothing more than a jumble of terms. Paired with their clues, though, each set kind of tells a story, with the answer finishing the tale.

#4—*Pick* me! I love doorknob locks. ANSWER: snake rake

#9—These chocolate-covered meringues are simply *köstlich*. ANSWER: schaumkuss

#11—For artists, drawing often *blurs the line* between work and play, but they don't let that _____ them. ANSWER: stump

#14—There's nothing *Smiley* about this cult-favorite horror franchise. ANSWER: Tooth

"Why are they making such a big deal over this new Puzzle Master?" I whisper. "You'd have to be a moron not to be able to answer these."

Then it dawns on me. You wouldn't have to be a moron at all. You'd have to be somebody . . .

"Somebody who isn't me."

Around the corner, I hear the muffled ding of the elevator arriving on our floor. Some sweaty guy in a rumpled shirt scurries off the elevator and into our office. He runs by with such fervor that my puzzles page goes flying.

"First-floor conference room, Junior. This one's a biggie."

Enzo doesn't even ask. He merely drops his drafting pencil, picks up a different pen and notepad, and sticks them in what I swear to potatoes is a *holster* on his belt. He must have rigged it especially for this purpose. If I weren't already quiet, I'd be speechless.

Enzo says nothing to me as he and the sweaty guy trot around the corner and recall the elevator.

You don't care about this job. You don't need it, I tell myself.

I can't bring myself to say I don't need *Enzo,* though.

I busy myself for a little longer, rotating the grid to see if there are any better ways to fit the tangle of squares onto the page. No matter what I do, it seems that there's only one configuration that will fit the space. I'm doing that thing where I let my focus blur, like I'm trying to see some sort of hidden picture in the mess of letters, and sure enough, I feel like I'm on the verge of seeing something. Two seconds more of staring at it, and I feel like it might reveal itself to me.

But I don't get that chance.

The ding of the elevator sounds from around the corner once again, and this time Enzo reappears.

His eyes are wide with news to share. There's something else in his eyes, though. Is that pity? I study his face, not sure. Then he says it all with one harrowing sentence.

"They found Mr. Gershowitz," he says solemnly.

From the way Enzo says it, I know immediately that means that they didn't find him alive.

I swallow hard. "Where?"

"The Golden Apple Factory," he says, "at the bottom of the peppermint vat."

CHAPTER 6

The buzz from offices on every floor of the *Banner* rises to the volume of a beehive. In less than twenty minutes, the story is writing itself. And I can hear it, word by painful word. I can hear all of it.

"What's the angle, Jerry? Another blow for the Golden Apple Corporation?"

"Nah, too dry. Nobody cares about a corporation. We need a *person*."

"We haven't got a person."

"Then we run with the Peterson angle."

"C'mon, we don't even know how much of that was Channel Four fluff."

"We need this story to *sing*, Tina. We haven't got time to triple-check sources."

I feel like I can't breathe. I need to leave. I think I'm going to vomit on the spot.

I make my way toward the door, but of course Enzo is already hanging in the threshold.

"Hey, we've still got tons of work to do!" he says. Guess I've found yet one more way to disappoint him.

"Puzzle's finished" is the only thing I can manage to say, and I point to my paper maze on the floor.

"You've still got to take that to the editor, and then to the art department, and then—"

"Enzo, *I need to go*," I say, and I can feel the food rise up in my throat.

I don't mean for it to sound so mean, and I guess it's a bad time, but I throw up on the carpet. Enzo glares at me, then at the mess I've made, and I can't tell if he's more embarrassed or sad. His face looks like I've lobbed a dagger straight into his gut, because Enzo actually doubles over a little. I should apologize, but the way those reporters were talking, the way they sounded so hungry for the story, so ready to make my dad the villain . . .

"I'll get some paper towels," I say.

"I'll clean it. Get some water," Enzo replies, though he says it to me like he's commanding a dog to go outside. And honestly, I kind of feel like a dog who peed in the house. I still feel sick.

As I lap up some water from the fountain outside, I spot Enzo wadding up paper towels in our office. I can't bring myself to go back and apologize, so breathless and sweating, I leave. I'm practically crawling by the time I reach my house.

Unfortunately, I'm not the only one there.

Detective Dale has my dad by the elbow, which is already a weird enough sight considering nobody could possibly have Dad's elbow unless Dad was *letting* them have his elbow. I square my eyes in on the scene and notice it's my mom who is putting up the fight.

"'Friendly chat,' my foot!" Mom exclaims, picking up her protest where she must have left it before I barged in. "There's nothing 'friendly' about any of this!"

"Diane," Dad says calmly, which is not a sentence I ever thought I'd write before.

"Ike was your friend!"

"Which is exactly why we think he can help shed some light on how this . . . tragedy . . . happened," Detective Dale says. He can't even feign sincerity.

Dad looks at Mom. "I'll be back before . . ."

But the word "dinner" trails off as we hear a noise sputtering outside. I turn to see a familiar black sedan roll over the loose gravel in the gutter.

Two pairs of shiny black shoes walk heel to toe on the asphalt, onto the sidewalk, up the drive, and come to a stop behind me.

"Detective Tapps," Dirk says, sliding his sunglasses down his nose and hooking them onto his suit pocket. "What an unexpected surprise."

Detective Dale's teeth close in a tight smile. "Yes, it appears this afternoon is full of, ah, *surprises*," he says, enunciating every word.

"We were just coming to have a word with our friend Mr. Peterson," says Bob.

The word "friend" sure seems to be getting thrown around freely today.

"Is that so?" says Detective Dale, his fingers curling a little tighter around my dad's elbow. Dad reflexively jabs the detective, who tries his best not to look bothered.

"It seems Raven Brooks's finest have made a rather unfortunate discovery at the Golden Apple Factory," Dirk says.

Unfortunate. Yeah, I suppose that's one way to describe finding a body at the bottom of the peppermint vat.

I can hear Detective Dale's teeth grind. "And how, might I ask, did you happen upon that bit of knowledge?"

Bob and Dirk exchange the smallest of smiles before Bob answers Detective Dale. "We have our sources. It seems the Raven Brooks Police Department has seen quite a bit of . . . *excitement* . . . these past few weeks."

Detective Dale's smile falls away, leaving behind only a set of bared teeth.

"I suppose condolences are in order," Dirk says to Detective Dale.

"Condolences?" he asks,

"Your demotion," says Dirk, taking obvious pleasure in the revelation.

"De-demotion?" Detective Dale's hand tightens around my dad's arm, but this time I don't think it's out of some weird display of power. I think he's trying not to fall over.

My mom has had enough.

"Now look here, *all of you*," Mom says, and where she's getting the chutzpah to lay into three detectives is beyond me.

"If you have a single, solitary reason to think that Ted has any information about how Ike Gershowitz, or *anyone*, died"—she eyes the German investigators—"then you can tell us what that is right now. Otherwise, come back when you have a warrant!"

I want so badly to bask in Mom's confidence. I wonder what

it feels like to be that sure of someone you love's total and complete innocence. But all I can do is look at Dad, and all he can do is look at me, because we both know that I left the tunnels with Ike Gershowitz's wallet, and we both know that same wallet is now in my dad's possession.

"I'll be back before dinner," Dad tells Mom again after the longest silence I've ever endured. His face is ashen, cheeks hanging like jowls. If he's eaten recently, I see no evidence of it.

After some terse debate, it's decided that Dad will ride in the back of Detective Dale's car, but the investigators will join in the "friendly discussion" at the police station.

I say nothing—I'm not sure if there's anything for me to say. All at once, I'm grateful that Mya is still confined to her room so that she didn't witness any of this.

After Dad leaves, I expect Mom will have something to say. Instead, she opens her mouth and waits, like she's hoping I'll have something to say instead.

When I don't, we both stare at each other for a moment, disappointed.

"It's going to be okay," I say uselessly.

"He'll be back before dinner," she says, her reassurance empty.

Then Mom motors over to the hall closet, where she keeps the phone book. She drops the spine of the thick book onto the table and

flips to the *L* section, running her finger down the page of splashy, full-color ads for lawyers. Then she starts dialing.

"Now, where was it I left off . . ." she mutters to herself. "There has to be a better option than that horse lawyer."

She's halfway through the second of what I suspect will be a long night of phone calls when I spot Mya at the top of the stairs, finally risking her punishment to see what's going on.

I can't hold it in any longer. I *need* to talk to Mya. I skip the steps two at a time before I meet her. Then I pull her into my room and throw the door shut behind me.

"Ow! I need that!" Mya says, yanking her arm from my grip. "And are you nuts, by the way? We're banned from speaking to each other, remember?"

"Mya! Mom's a little busy right now, and while you were holed up, you probably missed the big news—Dad's at the *police station being questioned*," I say.

I shove my hand into my pocket and pull out the gridded paper. If anyone at the *Banner* knew I'd taken an unpublished proof from the building, I'd be fired. But I've risked it already and spread the paper on the floor. I jam my finger down on the crossword.

"The Puzzle Master is talking to me."

Mya sits back on her heels and squints at me. "Like, he called you, or—?"

"No, of course not," I say.

"Right, that would be too obvious."

She's mocking me.

81

"Okay, so then what do you make of this?"

Mya cranes her neck to read the phrase I found at the *Banner*.

beware the Ravens They turn the tide

"Um. Well, the answers spell out a sentence . . . sort of . . ." she says, looking back down at the grid. "But it's not like the words make any sense together."

I shake her off. "You're getting hung up on the details."

"Details?" Mya throws up her hands. "It's seven words! I'd love details! Details would be fantastic! Where are the details?"

"Okay, first of all, *shh*," I say, pushing her hands down, and we both pause for a moment to make sure Mom is still yelling at lawyers on the phone. (She is.)

"Second of all," I say, then circle the first letter of each clue, eight through twelve. "How's this for details?"

Mya leans closer to the paper, and suddenly, she's not looking at me like I've lost my last marble. At least for a second. Then she's back to doubting me.

"It could be a coincidence."

"Aha!" I yell, and this time, it's her shushing me, but I'm hardly paying attention. Instead, I'm scrambling to my feet and digging through my other pants pocket.

"See, that's what I thought at first, too," I say, pulling out the other folded newspaper page so fast, I give myself a paper cut. "Then I remembered something."

I didn't register it at the time. Crossword puzzles were the farthest thing from my mind when I saw it. But some part of my subconscious retained it.

The discarded newspaper at Lucy's funeral, a half-completed crossword folded and forgotten.

"Look," I say, placing the edition in front of Mya. "Last week's paper."

Mya's finger traces the first letter of each word in clues eight through twelve.

Just like in this week's paper, the first letter of each of those clues spell the same name. *Mine.*

"This is huge!" she says.

"Yes! Finally! Thank you!"

Mya then points to the nonsensical string of words spelled out in the answers of the puzzle.

"beware the Ravens They turn the tide?" she says. "What kind of gobbledygook is that?"

We stare at the crossword with its coded sentence and the stacked letters that spell my name. We stare and then we stare some more. We stare so hard, the words start to blur and criss-cross one another.

"Tides . . . tides . . . like ocean tides?" Mya tries.

"Sure," I say. "Why not?"

"But ravens? What do they have to do with the ocean?"

We both think about it. Then Mya gets an idea. "The Puzzle Master picked you for a reason. So, all of this has to do with you. Or us. Or the Puzzle Master knows how much you know."

"Oh," I say, feeling a little silly. Every single clue seems to lead to an answer that's obvious to me, but maybe not to everyone.

"But then how do we know we can trust him?" I say.

Mya shrugs. "I mean, it does seem like he's trying to help us. Maybe that's why he's going to all the effort of hiding. Maybe he knows how much attention we've attracted by digging up all this Forest Protector stuff and Grandma and Grandpa's research."

My heart starts to race. Finally, the beginnings of a theory. "Then maybe we finally have someone on our side!"

Mya nods, and we each allow the tiniest of smiles to creep to our lips. For the first time in what feels like an eternity, we're approaching something that feels like hope. Even though, at the exact same moment as all this is happening, our mom's yelling at lawyers and our dad's somewhere in the Raven Brooks police station.

* * *

Dad doesn't come home the next morning.

It seems like Mom's forgotten all about our punishment. While she's on the phone with lawyer number eighty-six, Mya and I meet up with Enzo, Maritza, and Trinity at the Square. None of them look thrilled to see us.

"Sorry," I say first, which is a weird way to say hello.

"Glad you're feeling better," Enzo replies, though I'm not sure if he means it.

Unsurprisingly, there's no need to fill Trinity and Maritza in on the discovery of Mr. Gershowitz in the Golden Apple Factory. News that gruesome has a way of traveling fast—the *Raven Brooks Banner* has made sure of that.

"I just don't get it," Trinity says. "Why does everyone think your dad had anything to do with the accident?"

"*Either* accident," Maritza notes.

Enzo's face grows dark. "One accident is easier to explain away than two."

I eye my friend closely, looking for some sign of sympathy in that statement. I'm having trouble finding one.

Trinity looks up like she's about to say something, but her brow furrows as she spies something over my shoulder.

A cluster of maybe thirty people, among them Trinity's parents, have filed into the Square. They come armed with paper, thumbtacks, and tape.

"Remember to ask shopkeepers first," Mr. Bales says to the crowd. "Don't go wallpapering anywhere you please."

"Who would refuse?" someone asks, and others chirp agreement.

"Let's just try to remember what this is about," Mrs. Bales says, and the crowd calms a bit before dispersing like an army of ants.

Trinity gives her parents a little wave, then looks back at me, knowing an explanation is needed.

"The town wants answers," she says quietly. "My parents are the ones they trust to organize."

Mya cocks her head. "Answers?"

Just then, a volunteer whizzes by, shoving a flyer into my

Justice for Lucy

We the people of Raven Brooks, demand a COMPLETE, ACCURATE, and TRANSPARENT investigation into the events leading to the tragic loss of life experienced at the Golden Apple Amusement Park's Rotten Core attraction. Lucy Yi did not deserve to die.

The town of Raven Brooks DESERVES ANSWERS.

Join us at our JUSTICE FOR LUCY town hall, where we have invited city officials, Golden Apple Corporation executives, and police enforcement to present their findings and next steps.

HELP US KEEP THE NEXT TRAGEDY FROM HAPPENING!

NEXT SUNDAY AT 6P.M.

GOLDEN APPLE AMUSEMENT PARK AMPHITHEATER

hand before moving on to the next group of people enjoying their coffee at a nearby bistro.

The picture on the front is the same class photo of Lucy that's framed in the plaque at the center of the gaudy Golden Apple memorial behind us. Only on the flyer, her picture is much larger and centered prominently on the page.

JUSTICE FOR LUCY is typed in bold black letters above her picture, followed by a brief explanation.

On its surface, the effort is completely innocent. Noble, even.

But even though it's not technically written, I see my dad's name all over it.

Every demand, every bold word and exclamation point, seems to scream the name PETERSON. Enzo's words echo through my head again and again: *One accident is easier to explain away than two.*

A brief glance at my sister's stricken face is all I need to know I'm not the only one reading between the lines.

Another brief glance at our friends' lowered eyes is enough for me to know that they can say all they want that they're on our side, but what they *really* feel, what they *really* believe, is just one more puzzle I'm terrible at solving.

I feel like I'm going to throw up again.

"They think he did it," Mya says when we're home at night.

"Maybe not," I say, but she knows a lie when she hears one.

"It doesn't matter," I say. Another lie.

But even if we found proof that Dad is innocent, I doubt it could repair the damage that's been done. Now that there's a possibility we really are the evil, cursed family plaguing the town of Raven Brooks, there's no unringing that bell. The doubt was there when my grandparents were alive. It grew stronger when we moved here. The Channel Four news story practically etched it in stone.

Last time I checked, it was pretty hard to erase stone.

With Dad gone, and Mom otherwise unavailable, Mya and I decide another trip to the basement is our best shot at discovering the identity of the Puzzle Master.

The basement is more or less the way we left it the night Dad caught us. I know it's not possible after just a couple days, but I'm convinced there's a staleness in the air that wasn't here before.

"It's always weird looking for something we're not sure exists," Mya says, moving papers around on the desk.

"What I can't figure out," I say, joining Mya at the desk, "is why Dad seems to be making it harder for us to help him. If he'd just give us a clue—*anything* to let us know what he's been obsessing over down here—maybe we could actually bring him home."

"Dad? Be anything other than cryptic?" Mya laughs. "Mom

told me once he'd rather keep us locked up in a box, like toys on a shelf, than in danger. At least that way he'd know we're safe."

Safe? I can barely remember that version of my dad. These days, I'm not even sure he knows we live in the same house with him.

"What about that stack over there?" I say, pointing to a pile obscured under an open textbook on moon phases and ocean currents.

Mya lifts the heavy book but accidentally tips over the desk lamp, which sends pencils and rulers scattering and rolling to the floor.

Mya finds a brassy object the length of her palm, curled like a crescent moon, a pointy end on both sides. Close to one of the ends is a dark purple stone.

"Is that . . . ?"

I take the object from Mya's hand. She drops back to the floor, scattering the pages that fell until she comes up with three sheets of paper. She slams them down in front of the light.

The first page is nearly gray with pencil writing, eraser smudging, and hand smears. The writing I can make out is definitely Dad's, but it looks like he wrote it after drinking maybe twenty cans of soda. I can practically see burn marks on the paper from him writing so fast. The letters and numbers that reach every corner and edge of the paper are strung together in formulas, judging by the symbols connecting them, but it all looks like a secret, coded language.

The second page is something more familiar, and I recognize it immediately as a drawing of the device we found in the nest— the device that was stolen from this very office by Gordon Cleave.

Without meaning to, I glance up at the passage door to make sure it hasn't opened when I wasn't looking.

"Aaron, look!" Mya gasps.

She's looking at the third page, another drawing of the device. Only this one isn't a simple pencil sketch of the object. This is a deconstructed depiction of the device, each part broken out and labeled in detail. Lines point to components of the object and connect to labels like "sensor," "microfilter," "barometric pressure level," and "mercury reservoir."

One of the deconstructed parts looks identical to the one in Mya's hand.

I study the piece of metal and stone, and I don't know if it's the way it feels in my hand or if I'm getting a weird sixth sense for this sort of thing, but there's zero doubt in my mind that this piece is from the original object. Whatever Gordon Cleave meant to steal from this office that night, he didn't steal all of it. He left a piece behind.

I close my eyes and force myself to remember Opening Day, speeding past the accident and rewinding all the way to the moments before I followed Mr. Cleave into the tunnels.

He'd looked so anxious, so desperate to get Mayor Tavish's attention. He'd kept digging around in his pocket for something. It was the reason I followed him in the first place. I knew that whatever he was looking for, it was upsetting him that he didn't have it. Something had rattled his usual smugness.

And then finding him in the Observatory, his snarling face cursing my presence . . .

The graffiti all over the construction site while the Golden Apple Amusement Park was being built. *Cursed*. Wasn't that what was scrawled all over the place?

I look at Mya, suddenly remembering she's still there. She's looking at me like I've sprouted a tail.

"It wasn't the park that was cursed," I tell her, interrupting my own thoughts, and maybe I really have grown a second tail because I swear I see Mya taking a step toward the door.

And then there was the way Channel Four always seemed to get the scoop on every other news outlet in town. Their luck was bottomless.

Detective Dale's promotion on the police force.

Mr. Tavish's winning election for mayor.

"Then . . ."

I keep looking at Mya. She isn't seeing it. How is she not seeing it?

"Their luck ran out!" I say.

"Whose luck? What are you talking about?" Mya is beginning to look truly afraid of me, tail or not, so I make myself slow down.

"There's something about this device," I say, holding up the missing piece of Gordon Cleave's object. "It has something to do with luck. It's the reason Mr. Cleave and Mayor Tavish and Detective Dale—and who knows who else—all got what they wanted. The news story, the promotion . . . it's because they knew something about these devices that nobody else did."

Mya shakes her head. "But Channel Four went bust! And Detective Dale got demoted. And the Golden Apple Corporation is filing for bankruptcy."

I nod so hard, my head starts to hurt, but I can't stop. "Exactly! Which means something made their fortune turn . . ."

I'm right on the edge of it. An answer. An answer is finally coming.

"Turn . . . turn . . ."

I scatter the papers on the desk again, forgetting to be careful. I'm not worried about Dad finding out we were here. All I'm thinking about is confirming my suspicion.

Sure enough, under the same stack of papers Mya regathered from the floor, I find more of Grandma and Grandpa's pages, the very same pages he must have taken from my room. Each page contains at least some of the formulas on Dad's sheets. I glance to the book that tops the stack of papers, peering more closely at the page that's open.

Then I lift the left side of the book to view the cover. Its title reads: *The Mythic Tide: An Examination of Weather's Historic Connection to Fortune.*

"The Puzzle Master . . . what did he say?"

Mya's starting to get wide-eyed, too, and now we're both on the edge of an answer.

"They turn the tides," Mya says.

I turn the piece of the device in my hand, over and over like a wave rolling over sand. The deep purple of the gemstone near the tip catches the reflection of the lamplight, winking at me.

"He wasn't talking about ocean tides," I say, quietly at first, like I'm afraid I'll scare it away now that the solution is this close.

Mya turns back to the book Dad had opened to the moon phases page.

"That's what this book is about, though, isn't it?"

"I'm not saying that weather isn't involved. It is, somehow. But I don't think that's what the Puzzle Master was talking about."

I look deep into Mya's eyes. I need the courage to say it.

"I think he's talking about luck. Something in these devices helps people to change their luck."

"But Dad has one, and his luck couldn't get any worse."

"No," I say, holding up the metal crescent. "He has a piece of it . . . we only had the whole thing for a second. Before Gordon Cleave stole it back. Whatever it was doing up in that nest, it was bringing him his dose of luck. When we took it . . ."

"Everything fell apart," Mya finishes.

Then she drops her finger to the second sheet of pages she gathered from the floor.

"That's what Dad's been doing down here. He's been trying to re-create one of these devices."

Of course.

Mya falls into Dad's huge office chair, slumping and looking so much like him in this moment, it's a little unnerving.

"This is completely nuts," she says.

I lean against the desk and rock the lamplight, sending it swaying again.

"If we lived in a normal town with a normal life and a normal family," I say, "you'd be right."

"But we live in Raven Brooks," she says. "And we're Petersons. We can kiss 'normal' goodbye."

She looks so resigned to that fact. Something heavy settles in my stomach at the thought that my baby sister could be this defeated.

"Maybe we don't have to be cursed," I say, nodding to the crescent piece. "Maybe all we need is the right tools to change our luck."

I pocket the missing device piece and vow to keep it on me at all times from here on out. Right now, this bejeweled hunk of metal is the only thing keeping Mr. Cleave from regaining whatever power he used to have.

Just then, the muffled sound of the front door opening and closing drifts its way down to us through the insulated remove of the basement. A second later, the sound of Mom's voice shatters the quiet in the rest of the house.

"Dad," Mya and I say in unison, then scurry as fast as we can to switch off the light and close the office door behind us.

When we get to the top of the basement stairs, I open the door just a crack to see if I can detect where Mom and Dad are in the house. I'm startled to hear Dad's voice closer to the hallway leading to the basement than I'd expected.

I mouth the words "living room" to Mya, and she nods. Which means we have no choice but to hunker down here until Mom and Dad make their way to the kitchen so we can escape the hallway and sneak upstairs undetected.

When I hear the springs of the couch groan and settle, I make myself comfortable on the top basement step. We're likely to be here for a little while. Mya follows suit.

It isn't long before I wish we weren't stuck listening.

"It's absolutely absurd!" I hear Mom say. "It's like they want to blame you for everything from the dinosaur extinction to the Great Depression!"

"Diane, calm down."

Dad is calm enough for both of them. Except I don't think that's him being calm so much as bone-tired.

"I've *been* calm, Ted. That's *all* I've been."

Mya looks at me, cocking her head. *This is Mom being "calm"?*

"I haven't asked questions," Mom continues. "I haven't made waves. I haven't so much as blinked when you've stayed in the basement for weeks, barely eating, never sleeping."

"I know—"

"You *don't* know," Mom interrupts. She's had this saved up for three days. Honestly, it's amazing she hasn't burst into pieces by now.

"And up until today," she says, "I haven't known, either. I haven't known what's been eating at you, why we moved to Raven Brooks, what has you so worried. I haven't known why we had to leave Germany so fast—"

"You know why we had to leave Germany—" Dad insists.

"It was an accident. An *accident*, Ted. Nobody could have predicted what would happen that day."

"I could have."

"Then they should have listened to you. But that poor man's death is not on you. And neither was Lucy's."

I see Mya flinch at the mention of Lucy's name.

"It isn't that simple, Diane."

I can't tell if Dad is so much tired as he is completely incapable of making Mom understand. She only knows a fraction of what Mya and I have discovered, and it's hard enough for *us* to understand.

"Then make it simple," Mom pleads. "Tell me everything!"

There's a long, uncomfortable pause, and Mya and I lean closer to the door crack.

Then Dad says quietly, "I'm going to make this right. I'm going to rebalance the scales."

Mom sighs. "You know bloody well as I do that I don't know what that means."

"And that's the way it's going to stay."

"Ted, they're trying to take the house."

"This is my family's house," Dad chirps.

"Not according to the city. Something about unpaid property taxes dating back decades."

There it is again. More bad luck.

"That's impossible. My parents wouldn't have . . ."

"Let me guess, something else you can't tell me about," Mom says, a bite sneaking into her voice that wasn't there before. "At least this secret isn't a new one. If you had your way, I'd probably never know you *had* parents. You'd have me think you were hatched."

I hear the couch springs squeak again, and through the muffle of cloth or hair or grief, I hear Dad say, "I will make this right, Diane."

"Maybe some people just aren't meant to make it in this world," Mom says. "Maybe we're just spinning our wheels, trying to fight against fate."

After another long silence, Dad says, "Fate can be changed. Sometimes, all it takes is a spin of the dial for the whole tide to turn."

It's safe for us to get away. Mya and I spin on our heels, fast as we can to our respective bedrooms. But early into the gray hours of morning, I'm still staring up at my ceiling, replaying the night over and over, trying to make sense of the devices and the weather and the way they shift the tides of fortune, trying to unhear the confessions and fears of my parents and the curse of our family.

I want to stare out my window. When I can't sleep, sometimes I sketch the shapes I see in the clouds when they drift across the moon. But every time I look, all I see is the black car, parked across the street, in a spot just different enough to let me know it's being moved. The investigators are still watching.

CHAPTER 7

If anyone had asked me six months ago to name the person most likely to follow me into a burning building . . . well, I'd say Mya. But the second-most-likely person would be Enzo.

On second thought, Enzo's terrified of fire. Actually, he's terrified of everything. But he would have cared, at least. Like, *actually* cared.

Now it's like the person standing on the other side of our tiny desk at the *Banner* is a whole new person from the one I knew. A stranger.

"I just don't see why it's so important," Enzo says, scattering the crossword evidence I've just laid before him.

"Are you serious?" I say a little too loudly, and he looks up from his search long enough to scowl at me and close the door to our claustrophobic office.

"People are trying to work," he replies.

"Enzo, you said it yourself, it's weird. Why would this Puzzle Master ask for *me specifically* to be in charge of the crossword if he wasn't trying to send *me specifically* a message he doesn't want anyone else to see? Whatever he's trying to tell me must have something to do with *me* . . . or my family."

Finally—*finally*—Enzo gives up on his search for the elusive quote and looks at me with something resembling sympathy.

"Okay, I get it," he says.

I lower my eyes.

"Well, maybe I don't totally get it. I mean, my family isn't . . . I mean it hasn't been . . ."

Part of me wants him to just say it. Tell me what a mess my family is, how much we're hated, what everyone's really thinking. It would save me the pain of guessing all the time.

"Enzo," I say carefully, maybe because my feelings are hanging on by a thread here, "for the first time since we moved here, it feels like someone out there believes we're not evil. That maybe we're just . . . unlucky."

Lines form around Enzo's eyes, and for a minute, he looks so much older. Kind of like his dad.

"Not *everyone* thinks you're evil," he says, and I can't honestly tell if he's including himself in that "not everyone." There's that not knowing again. It hurts so much worse when the not knowing is about your best friend.

"Look," Enzo says, "I've tried to find out who the Puzzle Master is. I've been trying ever since the beginning of the summer."

"Seriously?"

"Of course 'seriously.' I mean, c'mon, you'd have to be dense not to at least wonder who the guy is."

"So then why is he such a mystery?" I ask.

"Because he *wants* to be," Enzo says. "I've never seen it before. The *Banner*'s treating him like a confidential source.

Only a couple of people know who he really is, and they're not saying a word."

"But he's not giving information on a news story," I say. "He's just—"

It finally hits me. From the look on Enzo's face, the answer just smacked him in the head, too.

"He's just feeding me information that could bring down some of the most powerful people in Raven Brooks," I say.

Enzo nods slowly before letting out a breath.

"If I ask my dad one more time about the Puzzle Master, he's going to start wondering why I want to know so badly," he says. The lines around Enzo's eyes return. "You're not imagining it," he says. "Everyone wants to blame your family."

He says it fast, like he's trying to let the truth escape.

"Or they want to blame *someone*," he says. "After Lucy . . ."

We both fall silent, just like everything falls silent around Lucy.

"People want a person to be responsible. They need to be mad at someone. The Yis don't have anyone to hate. Nobody knows how to get justice for Mr. Gershowitz, or heck, even *why* he had to die. The Golden Apple Corporation only cares about money and keeps trying to make candy. Did you know they've tried twice to reopen the park?"

I shake my head. No, I didn't know that.

"People call the *Banner* every day to yell at my dad about how the paper should be covering this more or that more, going after Mayor Tavish, going after the Golden Apple Corporation, going after your dad," Enzo says, leaving delicacy behind in the wake of his rant. "Dad's just trying to run the paper the right way. He's trying to be fair."

Enzo leaves it there, and I understand why. He wants me to know it's been a favor this whole time, that for weeks, Enzo's dad has been fighting to keep his eyes and the eyes of the *Raven Brooks Banner* focused on justice, not the town's appetite for vengeance.

But he can only hold off the masses for so long. Eventually, there'll be another Channel Four to rival the paper. Eventually, they'll be back to chasing leads and the splashiest stories.

"So, no more asking your dad about the Puzzle Master," I say, sinking into my chair.

"No more asking," Enzo says.

We sit in silence long enough to hear the rickety air conditioner kick on overhead.

"When one of my dad's editors told him about the Puzzle Master, my dad asked who recommended him. The editor said something about 'the weather wingnut,'" Enzo adds.

Weather wingnut? There's only one person in Raven Brooks I know who that could possibly be . . . Mrs. Ryland, our geography teacher.

"Bring your notebook," I tell Enzo. "I think I have a story."

* * *

First we need to grab our friends. We swing by Enzo's house for Maritza first and I'm taken off guard. I didn't know Trinity would already be there, planning a mural for Lucy.

"It's to make up for that horrible statue in the Square," Maritza explains.

It might have been petty, but I can't stop thinking about Mya. I know she's technically still grounded, but she was as close to Lucy as any of us—and she's not even involved in the mural.

"We need to bust Mya out of jail before we go anywhere," I say the second we get outside, and I'm relieved to receive zero argument on the matter.

"You know," Maritza says, "you two get grounded so often, one day we're gonna look up and be like, 'Has anyone seen Aaron or Mya? It's been like three years.'"

"Ha ha," I deadpan. "Hopefully it wouldn't take you three years to notice."

I wonder, though.

Jeez, how pathetic can I get?

It's hard not to feel a little sorry for myself, though, given that Enzo's basically just confirmed that Raven Brooks is a half step away from storming our house with torches and pitchforks.

By the time we arrive at my house, we have a loose plan to grab Mya.

"You're sure about the timing?" Trinity confirms.

"Trust me, every day at four o'clock, without fail. That dog is on a strict schedule."

Our plan hinges on our neighbor Mr. Quinn. I never thought I'd be glad to see him walking his mean schnauzer past our house, especially considering I'm always the one who ends up cleaning up that same mean schnauzer's poop because Mr. Quinn some-how magically never seems to notice that his dog takes a nice, long squat in the very same spot on our lawn. Every. Single. Day. Right at four o'clock.

Trinity and Enzo hide in the bushes beside my driveway while I climb the tree outside my window as quietly as possible. Maritza heads up to the hedge on the other side of the house and peeks around the corner before jerking back.

I hear a collar rattling in the distance, followed by the sound of Mr. Quinn's voice.

"Here we are, Tootsie. Just a little bit farther. You know what to do. That's right."

That's right, Tootsie.

I peer through the branches down at Maritza as she holds her palm up in a stop motion, shaking her head slowly.

"Okay, Tootsie-Pie. This spot looks good."

Wow. Not even trying to hide it anymore.

Maritza drops her hand just as the dog trots into sight on the sidewalk below. She steps backward through the bushes like a commando, and as quietly as possible, I slide my bedroom win-dow open and climb inside. I turn to make sure Mr. Quinn didn't see me, but he's too busy covering his own crime, looking twice over his shoulder toward our front door.

Just as Tootsie begins to squat, I see a ball bounce from the side of the house near my driveway and into the street, right across Tootsie's line of sight.

"No, no, Tootsie, leave it!" Mr. Quinn scolds, but it's too late. She might have had pooping on the brain seconds earlier, but the rainbow bouncy ball has taken total control, just as planned.

What wasn't in the plan was the gray neighborhood cat Trinity and Enzo must have scared out of the bushes shortly before they threw the ball.

"Tootsie, *NO!*" Mr. Quinn screams as Tootsie expertly slips through his grasp and redirects her attention to the cat, who's only just realized he's become part of a scheme he didn't sign up for.

The cat yowls, springing on all four paws like he's been electrocuted before darting across the street into the empty house's yard. Tootsie is hot on his trail, her leash flapping behind her like a cape. The ball is forgotten.

"Tootsie, you get back here this instant!" Mr. Quinn hollers, and finally, the commotion captures Mom's attention.

I hear the front door swing open, and soon, Mom is assessing the whole scene from the front stoop: the gray cat and his electric fur, the mean schnauzer and her remarkable prey instinct, Mr. Quinn and his strange surprise at Tootsie's viciousness.

This is my chance.

I race around the corner and burst through Mya's door without knocking, startling her from her study of our grandparents' notes.

"Hurry," I gasp.

"But Mom—"

"She's busy."

"Are you sure—?"

"Do you wanna argue, or do you wanna escape?"

Mya yanks her shoes on and follows me to my bedroom, witnessing the unfolding scene on the street for the first time.

The gray cat has made it up the trellis to the house across the way, but Tootsie isn't about to let that deter her. Somehow, she has managed to launch her schnauzer body high enough into the air to entangle herself and her leash below the cat, and if I didn't know better, I'd say the cat is taunting Tootsie just out of reach.

Still barking and snarling, the schnauzer is hopelessly stuck, a fact Mom seems to be aware of, but Mr. Quinn can't be convinced. He's yelling even louder than Tootsie.

"You get down from there right now, young lady! I'm warning you, it'll be a time-out when we get home!"

"Mr. Quinn, I think we might need to call the fire department," I hear Mom suggest. She's so calm when she says it, like calling the fire department is the easiest thing in the world. Which I guess, right now, it is.

"Do I even have time to ask?" Mya says.

"Nope. Just climb."

Mya's on the ground only seconds before me. We duck behind the hedge closest to Maritza, the safest place to hide until we can regroup.

It isn't until Mr. Quinn finally concedes and gets the fire department involved that we're able to make a break for it. The minute Mom goes inside to retrieve the phone, Trinity and Enzo sprint toward us. We weave in and out of neighbors' bushes and fences until we reach the end of the street and are in the clear.

"The cat was a nice touch," I say to Trinity and Enzo as soon as I regain my breath.

"I'm sure the cat would disagree," Trinity says.

"Does anyone want to tell me what's going on?" Mya says.

"We're going to find the weather wingnut," I say.

* * *

It's weirdly difficult to find a teacher's address in Raven Brooks. It's almost as though they don't want to be found.

"She's a big contributor to the Community Action Fund," Trinity says. "Mom and Dad say she's basically the only one who ever donates to the Emergency Preparedness Plan."

Which is how Trinity is able to get her hands on the address of Mrs. Ryland, geography teacher, Weather Lover, and apparently Emergency Preparedness Enthusiast.

"I mean, it makes sense," Enzo says. "If you're constantly ready for the Big One, I guess you'd want the rest of the town to be, too."

I have no idea how waiting for a giant earthquake makes Mrs. Ryland the only person in all of Raven Brooks who knows who the Puzzle Master is, but that hardly matters now. What matters is, she knows. And once I know, too, maybe I can finally figure out what it is he's trying to tell me.

We arrive at the curb of a small, one-story house, white-trimmed and bright blue, an overgrown flower garden spilling onto the sidewalk with weeds poking through patches in the grass. On our street the house would fit right in. A little shabby maybe, just enough to look lived-in, not neglected. On this street, though, every house is magazine perfect, flower boxes in every window, every picket of every fence soldier straight.

A woman in yellow rubber gloves crouches in the yard across the street, wielding a pair of pruning shears like a garden ninja.

"So, should we just knock, or . . ." Maritza says, and it occurs to all of us at the same time that we don't really have a plan now that we're here. Are we just supposed to ring the doorbell and demand the name of this crossword mastermind who has gone to such great lengths to remain anonymous?

The answer doesn't come from any of us, though.

"If you're looking for Rita, you won't find her topside."

It's the garden ninja across the street. I'd thought she was too focused on her begonias to notice us, but her eyes are trained on us now, clearly suspicious.

"Rita?" Enzo asks.

The lady eyes us more closely, squinting through the late-afternoon sun. She probably just realized we must be students, not small adults.

"Mrs. Ryland," she clarifies. "You won't find her in front of the house."

The woman returns to her pruning, apparently deciding we've been sufficiently dealt with.

Mrs. Ryland's backyard is a far cry from the front. Weeds and some overgrown grass might actually make it look better.

Two sprawling maple trees occupy the majority of the space, their leaves shading nearly every part of the patchy lawn that probably never had a chance to grow, given the jumble of cracked paving stones, discarded flowerpots, snarled vines tumbling out of untended planters, and a spigot slowly dripping water against the siding on the house, an orange rust stain carving a path down to the ground.

"Yikes," Maritza says. "I guess landscaping isn't really her thing."

Enzo picks up a rusted iron bistro chair that's tipped on its side, setting it beside the matching table randomly placed in the middle of the yard. A seat for one.

He slumps into the chair and surveys the backyard, and suddenly, I see his focus settle into the corner of the yard.

"What?" I say, trying to follow his gaze.

"That spot on the grass," he says, pointing with his chin to a place in the shade of one of the large maples.

"So?"

"Why is the grass so green there?"

I peer closer at the spot in the yard I could have looked at a hundred times and missed. It's impossible not to see the difference now that Enzo has shown me.

The five of us crowd around the circle of grass the size of a manhole cover. Trinity crouches to run her hand over the surface.

"It's fake!"

We all follow suit, letting the unmistakable feel of artificial turf tickle our palms.

"It's like a mini golf green," Mya says.

"What was it the neighbor said about 'topside'?" I say.

Enzo parts the real grass from the fake stuff and finds a clear separation.

And a hinge.

"No way."

I shrug. "I mean, is it really that hard to believe?"

Enzo curls his fingers and raps on the ground covered with fake grass. His knock echoes back against a metallic surface.

There's a brief pause while we all consider what we've just discovered.

Then, an answer from below: "No."

Mrs. Ryland sounds like she's on the other end of a very long, tin chute. It reminds me of the way Mya and I used to see if it was really possible to thread a string between two cups and actually hear each other. Usually, it was just us yelling really loudly into empty soup cans.

She actually gives in a little easier than I expect her to, and with a sound like the hydraulics of a bus lowering to the curb, Mrs. Ryland's hatch door swings open, nearly whacking Mya in the nose.

Besides a narrow ladder, we can't see a thing beyond the deep, dark hole where Mrs. Ryland is apparently residing over summer break.

Enzo gestures gallantly to me. "By all means."

"Gosh, thanks," I say, frowning at him. "Generous of you."

"Hey, it's your Puzzle Master, not mine."

I step onto the ladder and begin my descent, the metal shaft a little close for comfort. The deeper underground I go, the less I like this idea, and the more this place reminds me of a different set of tunnels.

It occurs to me a little too late that I don't exactly know what

Mrs. Ryland's connection to this whole thing is. It seems unlikely that she could have anything to do with Mr. Cleave or Detective Dale or any of the others who secretly gather in the Observatory. It seems almost impossible that she could be at all a part of whatever got Mr. Gershowitz killed.

Almost.

By the time I reach the end of the ladder, the chute has widened to a landing big enough to hold the five of us, but just barely. The only opening from here stands about two feet off the ground. We have to move one by one on our hands and knees through it.

"This had better be worth it," Maritza says, and I couldn't agree more.

Nothing could have prepared me for what awaits us at the end of the metal tunnel.

It's an entire house packed into one round room.

There's a small living room with a coffee table over an oval rug, an overstuffed wing chair with a cane-shaped lamp over its shoulder. There's a kitchenette with a tall, slender refrigerator, a short countertop surrounding a narrow sink, and a two-burner stove beside a cubicle microwave. There's a Murphy bed peeking out from a large cabinet scooted against a bowed wall. There's a door partially obscuring a bathroom sort of like the one I saw in the sleeping car of a train once in Germany, complete with an over-the-toilet shower nozzle and a pocket-sized sink jutting from the wall.

If not for the fact that we're easily twenty feet underground—or the hard-to-miss metal rack of about a thousand cans and jars of food taking up roughly half of the bunker—I might think we were in an actual house. A very small house.

Somehow, I nearly missed Mrs. Ryland standing there in the center of the bunker with her arms folded tightly across her chest, lips pursed.

"Lovely. You've brought an entire crew."

She sighs, turning her back and flitting to the kitchenette. She flings open one of the two cabinets affixed to the wall, then sets mason jars on the countertop.

"Sit down. I'll pour you something to drink. But take off your shoes at least."

We do as we're told; Mrs. Ryland is still a teacher, after all. We search awkwardly for a moment before each finds a place on the rug, none of us wanting to occupy the only chair in the whole bunker.

Mrs. Ryland makes three trips to the coffee table, setting down jars of thick orange drinks that smell like a mix between beets, carrots, and grass clippings, a cluster of mysterious yellow flecks floating toward the foamy surface.

"Thank you," we all say, no one wanting to take the first sip.

At last, Mrs. Ryland falls into the wing chair. We've already exhausted her.

"Well, then?" she says, eyeing each of us.

I'm desperate to jump straight into my questions, but judging by the expression on everyone else's faces, it looks like we might have to address the elephant in the room first.

"This is a . . . er . . . lovely . . . habitat you have here," I say.

Enzo looks at me like he's embarrassed for the both of us. "Habitat?"

"Well, what would you call it?" I mumble through gritted teeth.

"I love how you've, um, decorated," Trinity attempts before taking a sip of our orange-beet surprise.

"It's cozy," Maritza adds.

Mrs. Ryland shakes us off. "It's a fully functioning, self-sustaining shelter customized specifically to support a single life up to a full year in the event of imminent disaster," she says as though it's the most normal thing in the world to be spending her summer in a deep hole under her backyard.

"That's . . ."

Brilliant.

Impressive.

Frighteningly paranoid.

"Neat," I say.

"Neat," she says, lids half-closed over her eyes.

But I have more important topics for discussion.

"Mrs. Ryland," I say, "I need to know who the Puzzle Master is."

It wasn't exactly my strategy to catch her off guard, but now that I have, I'm able to see the split second Mrs. Ryland decides to lie to me.

"Who?" she says coolly.

I lean over the coffee table toward her overstuffed chair.

"You heard me," I reply.

She blinks.

I blink.

Enzo tries his drink and audibly gags.

Then, with startling efficiency, Mrs. Ryland stands from her chair and flips a switch on the wall. Without warning, the lights in the bunker shut down, and I hear the hatch door swing shut with an echoing clang. The room re-illuminates, only this time with an eerie blue glow, and it takes me a second to realize that the glow is coming from a newly exposed wall, covered floor to ceiling with monitors, switches, hard drives, and dials. A steady *bloop* accompanies one of the flashing dots on the primary monitor, showing a heat map of the entire world that finally brings the whole picture into focus. I exhale as I realize what's going on.

Mrs. Ryland is operating her very own weather station right here in her one-person bunker. She's waiting for the Big One, an earthquake, and when the Big One finally does hit, she'll be the lone survivor among a town of fools.

"Who sent you?" Mrs. Ryland says, narrowing her eyes at me. Her nose is inches from mine, and I can smell the peanut butter she must have had for lunch.

"What?" It's all I can manage.

"Who are you working for?" she demands, her eyes so squinty, I wonder if she can even see me.

"Uh—"

"How do I know the Ravens haven't gotten to you? Did they send you to find me?"

The . . . what? Mrs. Ryland is making less sense than usual. Her eyes twitch from one corner to the next.

"I knew I should have swept the place for bugs. They must have been listening in this whole time," she mumbles to herself.

I turn to Enzo for help, but he's never looked more clueless. Trinity and Maritza look to each other. It's Mya who finally comes to my rescue.

"Mrs. Ryland, that equation—what does it mean?"

Mya is making her way toward the wall of dials and maps, and at first, Mrs. Ryland looks like she might lunge at my sister. But when she sees what it is Mya is pointing to—a digital representation of numbers and letters that look vaguely familiar—she slows her walk toward Mya and stares dreamily at the formula.

"Why would you want to know that?" Mrs. Ryland says, suspicion still apparent in her voice.

"Because I've seen it before," Mya says. "In my grandparents' notes. It occurs again and again in their old binders. I must have seen it a dozen times."

Suddenly, despite the blue glow of the room and the steady *bleep* of her monitors, Mrs. Ryland's guard falls. Her face softens as she stares at my sister.

"Your grandparents," she says, like she's just now put two and two together. "Child, don't you have any idea what it is your grandparents were trying to do?"

"No."

It isn't just Mya. It's not just me, either. We all say it. In unison, the five of us, on the brink of finally knowing.

Mrs. Ryland shakes her head slowly.

"I suppose your parents would want to protect you," she mutters. "If *they* even knew, that is."

Mrs. Ryland takes a long, deep breath and meanders back to her chair. We all follow like ducklings.

"Your grandparents were brilliant," she says to Mya, then to me. "Every Peterson I've ever crossed paths with is brilliant, in fact. I know you've heard at least that much before, but let me tell you, I haven't even begun to scratch the surface of their findings, and I've been studying for decades."

"I don't get why that would be so dangerous," Maritza says.

Mrs. Ryland looks at her, deadly serious. "Weather is a dangerous business."

Enzo snorts beside me, and I jab him with an elbow before Mrs. Ryland continues.

"Adelle and Roger came to Raven Brooks to study its unique weather properties, to try to understand the cause of the phenomena that only seemed to affect this town."

"Right, and they died before they could," Mya says.

"No," Mrs. Ryland interjects. "They *did* find the cause. That's why they were stopped."

"Stopped?" Enzo says, clearly doubting Mrs. Ryland's weather conspiracy.

Mrs. Ryland continues. "They discovered a nest—"

"So did we!" Trinity pipes in, and this captures Mrs. Ryland's attention.

"I hope for your sake you left it undisturbed," she says, and we all fall quiet. It's not exactly a lie if we don't admit the truth.

"What they discovered in that nest," Mrs. Ryland continues, "was that."

She points to the formula Mya indicated on the wall.

"Whatever was in that nest was key to the weather phenomena in Raven Brooks. What you found in your grandparents' notes is the mathematical composition of whatever it was they discovered in the nest before . . ."

"Before . . . ?" I prompt as Mrs. Ryland hesitates.

She sighs impatiently. "Back then, the Tavish family ran this entire town. It still does, in a way."

I picture Mayor Tavish in his ridiculous tuxedo and top hat on Opening Day, the way he stood on a box to look taller. But then I recall the way my dad—the strongest, most intimidating person I know—doing this little man's bidding.

"Your grandparents' research was funded by the Tavishes, among other rich and powerful people in Raven Brooks," Mrs. Ryland continues. "Whatever they found in that nest had something to do with the anomalies they'd been studying, and apparently, they discovered more than they were supposed to."

I hear Mya's throat click as she swallows. "What happened to them?"

"Arrested," Mrs. Ryland says without hesitating. "The first of many times, from what I gather, all after getting a little too close to something they weren't supposed to find." She

points back toward the equation on the wall. "That, along with some rudimentary sketches, was all they could note before police dragged them away from the nest, accusing them of trespassing on Tavish land. Then, of course, the nest disappeared."

Mrs. Ryland's eyes go glassy. "They always disappear."

"And let me guess," Enzo chimes in. "One arrest too many, and suddenly, their funding went away. No money, no studies, no studies, no discoveries."

Mrs. Ryland nods slowly. "When the university first hired them to study the weather occurrences, I don't suppose the Tavishes ever imagined they'd get as close as they did to answers."

She returns her focus to Mya and me. "Your grandparents were something else," she says, and I hear the sadness in her voice, something close to regret.

"It's easy to become the town nutcase," she says.

"That's why they were blamed for the Factory fire," Maritza replies.

Mrs. Ryland's shoulders fall. "It's so much easier to believe in two bitter scientists than an entire conspiracy of Ravens."

There it is again, the Ravens.

Mrs. Ryland seems to anticipate my question. "The rich and powerful—they're the Ravens. The rest of us are just crows." She goes foggy again. "And the Ravens always hold the power."

Suddenly, her focus returns, and her words are more urgent. "I don't know what you kids have stumbled onto, but whatever it is, I don't want any part of it."

"We need—" Trinity interjects.

"What you *need* is to back as far away from this whole mess as you can. Trust me, this can only end badly."

"Welp," Enzo says, springing to his feet. "That's all I needed to hear." He pivots to me. "You can stick around if you want, but I've had enough."

Maritza and Trinity nod in wide-eyed agreement. "Let's go, Aaron," says Trinity.

I look to Mya. She drops her head, defeated. "We'll have to find another way," she whispers, then quickly follows the others through the passage leading to the stairs.

I take two steps toward the passage, but it's like my shoe is stuck to the ground or something, refusing to let me go.

"I came here for a reason," I tell Mrs. Ryland, but she's already scooping up our untouched glasses of carrot grossness.

"And now you can leave with that reason," she says, her voice a weird sort of forced relaxed, like she's trying to tell herself the threat is gone. But I'm still here.

"I need to know who the Puzzle Master is."

Mrs. Ryland grows still for just a second, then resumes rinsing glasses.

"Not a clue what you mean," she says.

"Mrs. Ryland, please," I say. "He's trying to tell me something. I need to be able to talk to him. *Really* talk to him."

She sighs, turns fast, and closes her eyes while she talks. "If he wanted that, do you think he would have gone to all the trouble to hide his identity?"

I stay where I am. I can out-stubborn her.

She tips her head back in utter exasperation. "Look, if I knew his name, I'd tell you," she says, talking to me like I'm a grown-up. "I'd tell you anything to leave. The longer you pester me in here, the more danger you put both of us in."

For the first time since entering Mrs. Ryland's emergency shelter, my blood runs cold, which maybe should have happened sooner, but let's face it, I've seen some pretty messed-up stuff over the past several months. It takes a lot to faze me anymore.

"I have to find him," I say, pleading.

She furrows her brow. "Then send him your own message!"

"Huh?"

"You heard me. Stick your own clue in the crossword. Don't you people work at the paper?"

Of course. I can't believe it never occurred to me. The crossword not only can be a two-way channel; it *is* a two-way channel.

"Mrs. Ryland, you're a genius," I say.

"I know!" she exclaims, throwing her hands in the air. "Now get out of my bunker!"

I leave without even thanking her. I think the leaving was thanks enough. No sooner does my foot rise off the last rung of the chute than the hatch door slams shut, narrowly missing my heel.

The others are waiting on the curb, heads in hands, exhausted by conspiracy.

"What?" Enzo says, the first to turn and see my face, which must be the picture of pure mania by the way he's looking at me.

"We need to get back to the *Banner* office," I say, and Enzo presses his head between his hands.

"*Now* you want to work all of a sudden," he laughs.

I know he's still mad at me for not taking the job at the *Banner* seriously enough. I know his patience is growing thin with me. I know there's something else, something I can't quite pinpoint—or maybe I don't want to pinpoint—that's pressing a wedge between us.

But none of that matters at this moment because I'm so close to meeting the Puzzle Master. I can feel it.

I'm so close to getting the answers that could make the difference between my family's safety—or total ruin.

* * *

With Enzo grudgingly standing guard to ensure no one sees me messing with the final proof of tomorrow's edition, I pull the crossword and painstakingly rework it, making all the pieces fit around the spaces for the answer I know the Puzzle Master will get.

Then I place my clue: "Once Upon a _____ Dreary + a domesticated camelid."

CHAPTER 8

Later that night, Mya and I hatch a plan to find the Puzzle Master with the clues I left. But eight minutes to midnight, I'm positive we're going to be late to the llama farm.

"Would you relax?" Mya huffs away next to me, struggling to keep up.

"We should have just chanced it," I say.

"Are you joking?" Mya screeches. "If you think I'm stepping foot in those tunnels again, you're dumber than I thought."

I don't know why I'm blaming Mya. If I'm being totally honest, I would do anything to avoid getting anywhere near the tunnels ever again. It's just that I'm so close to meeting the Puzzle Master and maybe—possibly, *finally*—getting answers to the biggest questions I have, answers that could prove Dad's innocence and make the people of Raven Brooks realize our family isn't the three-headed beast sent from another dimension to wipe Raven Brooks off the face of the earth they think we are.

"Do you realize that half the summer is already over," Mya reflects, "and we've spent, like, ninety-eight percent of it sneaking out in the middle of the night?"

"What can I say? I'm a great influence," I reply.

If I'm being honest, though, I'm not proud. The weight of tonight is starting to press down on me. There's so much at stake, it's enough to crush a person. If that weren't enough, there's so much that could go wrong. Like:

The Puzzle Master could leave before we even get there.

Maybe he never got the message at all.

We could be followed. It's not like it hasn't happened before.

And who's to say the Puzzle Master can actually be trusted?

When we arrive, I'm struck by how quiet and peaceful the llama farm is at night. Not that I spend much time on llama farms, but I seem to recall farms in general being bustling places, alive with constant work and animal grunts.

Mya and I stand on the edge of the farm, looking at each other like maybe the other person knows what to do next.

Then the grass nearby is disturbed, and the sound of rustling makes its way toward us. I push Mya behind me, but the sound is too close. We don't have time to run.

From around a ramshackle wooden barn emerges a llama, sleepy-eyed like we've just woken him up. He's chewing slowly, eyes glancing at each of our hands like maybe we have something for him.

Mya exhales hard. Or maybe that was me.

"I don't suppose you brought him anything?" she says, looking sorry for the llama.

"No, llama snacks weren't exactly top of mind when we snuck out," I say dryly.

She purses her lips and fishes in her pocket, inexplicably pulling from it two halves of a carrot, peeled and washed.

The llama wastes zero time. She giggles as his mouth tickles her palm, and when he's done, Mya finds the question on my face.

"Sometimes I get hungry," she says defensively.

"So, you just walk around with carrots in your pockets all the time?"

"Not *just* carrots," she says like *that's* the weird part.

One mystery at a time.

When we hear another rustling farther away, neither one of us reacts at first, thinking it must be another llama catching wind of the midnight snacks on offer. When the first llama isn't joined by a friend, however, Mya and I inch a little closer to each other.

"Maybe a raccoon?" Mya whispers, but neither of us believes that.

Mya and I try to duck just in case, but it doesn't matter. Whoever is there has surely already seen us.

Pressed against the ramshackle barn and crouched low in the tall grass, we wait for the brush to stop moving. When it finally does, instead of anyone emerging, the night once again goes still.

"I don't like this," I whisper to Mya. "Something feels off."

We stare again at the now-motionless scene and consider all the horrifying possibilities. What if someone else decoded my message to the Puzzle Master? What if it isn't him at all who's here to meet us? What if we're walking straight into a trap?

"We should go," I say to Mya, and she doesn't argue. Instead, she keeps low in the grass and begins moving sideways like a crab toward the road.

Just then, a sound not unlike the squawk of a crow pierces the air.

Mya turns back to me.

I shake my head. I have no idea. It might have been just a bird.

But why did it sound like a person making a bird noise?

And we're back to bird people again.

There's no doubt in my mind that the sound is directed at us.

I look to Mya, and she's shaking her head, already sensing that I want to investigate. She's right, of course. I'd be out of my mind to walk toward the obviously human-made sound. I'm pretty sure this is the very picture of BAD DECISION.

Except I have this nagging feeling it isn't a trap. None of this is. I think—heck, I think it's the Puzzle Master.

I move away from my sister and toward the thicket, distancing myself from Mya.

I move along the fence, staying low even though I've clearly already been spotted. The closer I get to the tangle of overgrowth where I heard the cawing, the harder my heart throbs. Is it the Puzzle Master? Or certain doom? Either way, something big is about to happen . . . even if I could be meeting my end.

"Hello, Aaron Peterson," a voice says.

CHAPTER 9

"**Y**ou named the cat Jinx," the voice continues.

What?

"You named him Jinx. You told him you two were the same, gray-like shadows, living in the unluckiest of all places."

He's talking about one of the neighborhood cats that stalks our yards and annoys the dogs, the one I talk to when I'm alone. I didn't think anybody knew that. How did he?

I step toward the voice to find someone not much bigger than me in size and stature. He's small to the point of looking almost frail, with glasses too big for his face on his slender nose. He wears a windbreaker and pants even though it's summer, and though his hair tries to hide underneath a baseball cap, there's only so much unruliness a hat can hide. What I notice most about him, though, is his hands. They're large for his body, with long knobby fingers that curl like they haven't relaxed in some time. The arms and shoulders they're attached to are just as tense. His shoulders form a perfect *M* behind his head, burying his neck.

"You've been watching me," I say, and I can't decide whether to be terrified or furious.

"Yes," he says with stunning honesty.

I take a few more steps toward him, and he cowers, seemingly out of impulse, before facing me again defiantly, though still on the ground, leaning backward to look up at me.

"Why have you been watching me?"

He takes a deep, impatient breath. "Because we need each other, Aaron Peterson. And I knew you wouldn't trust me at first."

Mya is behind me now, having decided that either it was safe or that I needed backup. I'm still not certain which is true.

"Prove it," I say. "Prove you're the real Puzzle Master."

He takes a single step toward me now, as though to even the score between us.

He reaches into one of the many zippered pockets of his tattered windbreaker and pulls out a cylindrical object the size of a lip balm case. When he hands it to me, I turn it over a few times. Then I realize that the cylinder is actually a stamp, made of wood everywhere except for one end, which is covered in ink-stained rubber. The grooves of the rubber match the seal on the Puzzle Master's letters.

I hand it back to him slowly, and he takes it more gently than he handed it to me, before returning it to the safety of his pocket.

"I wasn't spying," he says, very agitated. He keeps looking over his shoulder like he expects to be taken down by a rabid llama.

"I was surveilling you," he continues, and clearly the distinction is an important one to him. "You had to become the designer of the page so that you could complete the real puzzle."

"Finding the messages in the crossword," I say, and like a cog in a gear, realization clicks into place.

For the first time, the man actually looks satisfied, like my brain is finally working at his speed.

"There was only one configuration that would work in the space allotted on the page. I made sure of that."

"How . . . how could you possibly know how much space they'd have?" Mya says, and the man is back to looking over his shoulder.

He lowers his voice even more and leans toward us both.

"Because I used to work for the *Banner*. A long time ago."

I stare at him like I should know him somehow. It's bizarre how a perfect stranger could seem almost familiar.

"Who are you?" I say, then hold my breath.

The man stares at us both for an eternity. "My name?" he says, and it sounds like he hasn't said it in what must be thirty years. "My name is Norman Darby."

"Wait," I say, a memory floating back to me from the dredges of my mind. "Darby . . ."

He waits for me. I wonder if he's testing me, too. Making sure I'm really going to be of any use to him.

Finally, the memory drops, a little firework show going off in my brain. I was in Mrs. Ryland's class, conspiracy theories swirling like tiny tornadoes.

My evil grandparents.

Forest Protectors.

Factories on fire.

And a rogue reporter who was fired, then disappeared.

"You're that reporter!" I say, and Norman Darby's eyes glow like the light bulb is going off in his head instead of mine.

"*Investigative* reporter," he says, correcting me like I should be calling him Doctor Darby.

He rolls his shoulders back. "Researching you was part of my job. The most important job of my career, in fact."

There go his glowing eyes again, and Mya cuts in before we can travel too far without her.

"Someone going to fill me in?" she says, sounding more like a little sister than I've heard lately.

"He reported for the *Banner* back when Grandma and Grandpa were at the height of their research," I explain to Mya. "He wrote about the rumors going on in Raven Brooks, the same types of stuff Grandma and Grandpa were studying. The weather patterns, the nests, the birds—"

"Not rumors," he says, crossing his stiff arms across his chest. "I'm not a gossip columnist, thanks very much."

"Sorry, I didn't mean—"

"Your grandparents were right on the verge of a massive discovery, and I was the only reporter they trusted to help them expose the secret."

Suddenly, it's like the dam that's been holding all my questions has broken.

"It started with the nests," he continues, eyes darting back and forth between Mya and me. "By some miracle, they managed to find one and excavate it before it disappeared."

"So did we!" Mya contributes excitedly, but Norman shoves past me and holds her by the shoulders.

"And this is exactly why you're in danger," he snarls.

I pull Mr. Darby away and steady him—or maybe steady myself—against that dire warning. There's so much more to ask.

"We already know they found one of the devices," I say, and Mr. Darby's wild eyes lock on mine again.

"They didn't just find one. They learned what it does."

"What . . . what does it do?" I stutter. I am practically coming out of my skin.

Mr. Darby's voice drops to a whisper. "It turns the tides."

Mya groans behind me. "No more riddles. Please!"

Mr. Darby looks confused. "It's hardly a riddle," he says.

"It changes luck," I say, "like the tides of fortune."

Mr. Darby nods rapidly. "Yes, but *how*?"

He doesn't wait for me to answer.

"Haven't you noticed how the weather fluctuates? Just who do you think has been manipulating that?"

"But I thought the devices were like weather detectors. There's that sensor in there," I say.

"Exactly!" says Mr. Darby. "They detect the weather, but that isn't all they do. That merely tells them when to perform the ceremony. The real action begins when they harness the electro-magnetic activity!"

"Electro what now?" I say.

Mr. Darby races ahead. "Your grandparents, they explained it to me once, but of course they knew a great deal more. I only needed to know enough to write my exposé. But I do know this:

It's less about the devices, and more about *who* controls the devices."

My hands suddenly start to sweat. I'm thinking back to being thrust back into the tunnels, searching in the dark for Mya while at least three angry pairs of feet slap the cold, hard tunnel floor close behind me. I'm pressed against the curved corridor wall, inches from being found in the pitch black.

"Detective Tapps," I say. "I know Dale Tapps is one of them. And Cleave."

Norman Darby's face darkens. "Cleave," he says, teeth gritted against a deep, dark memory I can't see.

I begin to ask, but Mya puts her hand on my shoulder lightly. We should wait.

"He was my editor at the *Banner*," Mr. Darby says. "Mean, but not just mean. Cunning, but not just cunning. He was always scheming, always manipulating. The worst kind of cruel."

We listen.

"I got too close," he says, though I can tell his eyes are traveling. "I had no way of knowing what he was part of."

I want to shake Norman, get him to be somehow less cryptic. I'm not sure how much more of this I can take.

Suddenly, the rustle of grass snaps all three of us to a halt. We stand motionless, searching for the sound's source, and it doesn't take long to find the deep bends in the grass as someone makes their way toward us. There's nothing stealthy about the movement. It's almost like whoever is approaching doesn't think it's at all weird that three people are creeping around a farm in the middle of the night, whispering about conspiracies.

Which can only mean that . . .

"We were followed," I whisper.

Then, through the separation in the tall grass, a llama strolls straight into our secret meeting. It's the same llama Mya fed carrots to.

"Oh, hey, buddy!" Mya says.

"Shoo!" I say, angry at the interruption and definitely not angry at myself for being afraid of a llama.

"Sorry, I don't have any more carrots," Mya says to the llama, and I swear he understands, because he turns and walks away just as casually as he arrived.

Mr. Darby blinks after it. "They sound quite human in their gait, don't they?"

"Mr. Darby," I say, desperate to bring us back to the whole reason we're here. "What are Mr. Cleave and Detective Tapps and all the rest so afraid of us finding out?"

Mr. Darby actually looks confused, like he can't believe I haven't figured it out by now.

"They're a society," he says, bewildered at me. "They wear the feathered robes as part of the ritual, but over time, they've managed to somehow create a myth around it. You might have heard of it—"

"Forest Protectors," Mya says.

"A myth frightening enough to scare people away from the truth," Mr. Darby says. "The devices are old, perhaps even ancient. It's likely that whoever discovered them did so at the same time they discovered the tunnels. Whatever the origins, it's clear that the tunnels, the Observatory, and the devices are all spokes on the same wheel."

"So, whoever holds the devices receives the fortune?" I say.

"Theoretically, yes," Mr. Darby says.

"Then why not just steal all the devices, drop them in a pile, and smash them to bits? Problem solved," I say.

"It isn't that simple," Mr. Darby says, looking a little scandalized. "Whatever properties these devices hold, they maintain a delicate balance. One disruption to the balance and the entire thing falls apart. I cannot emphasize enough how dangerous it is to toy with the balance. There's simply too much we don't understand about it. Your grandparents knew that. To this day, I have no idea what happened to the device they did find. All I know is that they didn't have it when they died. They made sure of that."

"Why me, though?" I say, one of my biggest questions still unanswered.

Mr. Darby surprises me with a quiet, unpracticed smile. "You're a Peterson. There isn't a single part of this conspiracy that doesn't somehow touch you. And that's why I trust her, too." He motions to Mya. Then he adds, "Some people inherit money, houses, the whole nine yards. For you kids? This is your family's legacy. Your inheritance."

He lets that sink in a moment before finishing his thought. "Your grandparents taught me that messing with mysterious phenomena brings unpredictable consequences."

In layman's terms, something went wrong, likely with one of the devices.

Mya's hand brushes against mine, imperceptible to Mr. Darby. She's remembering the same thing that I am—the piece of Cleave's device we found in Dad's office.

Except that Dad's luck seemed to run out long before the device broke apart.

"That still doesn't explain why we're so . . . cursed," I say.

"Not all bad fortune is mystical," Mr. Darby says. "This society, they'll stop at nothing to protect their secret. Those of us who have gotten too close . . ."

Mr. Darby goes quiet, and I run through the list in my head.

Grandma and Grandpa, with their ruined careers and shattered reputation.

Norman Darby with his lost job and exile to reclusion.

Our family, with Dad's investigations, the weight of death pushing heavier and heavier on his shoulders.

"I've entrusted my knowledge to a select few—Mrs. Ryland, an old friend from my early reporting days; a fellow by the name of Roth; and of course Ike Gershowitz, family friend to the Petersons. Mrs. Ryland lives between her bunker and masked by a charade of, well . . . whatever you want to call it."

A recent memory surfaces, one of Maritza recalling the time Mrs. Ryland won a favor from Mr. Esposito. He must have paid her back with anonymity.

"And we all know what happened to poor Ike," Mr. Darby says.

"We do," Mya says, looking afraid for the first time tonight.

Mr. Darby does nothing to assuage her fear. "As old as these tunnels and the devices are, one thing remains clear—the town of Raven Brooks was built on a conspiracy of Ravens."

Raven Brooks. *That must be why it's named what it is.*

"And we're all just crows," Mya says.

"I see your sister got your grandparents' intellect," he says.

The grass crackles again, and the llama returns, hopeful that the snacks have somehow regenerated in Mya's pocket.

"Ugh, be gone, llama!" I say. My head's starting to hurt.

I'm not the only one who's reached his limit, though.

"I can't stay any longer. I might have been followed," Mr. Darby says. "And you two also. Watch your backs. If it was easy for me to track you through the woods, it would be easy for them, too."

"It was *you* chasing us to the Factory that night?" I say.

"My apologies, but I needed you to see what you saw," Mr. Darby replies.

"We were already going there," I say, annoyed. "We would have seen it anyway."

"But what you didn't know was that the meeting of the Ravens was about to end. Had you not made it through the basement and into the darkness of the tunnels, you might have been caught in the basement. Caught by *them*. And who do you think helped?"

"Oh," I say, feeling a little sheepish. I know I should say "thank you," like Mom would want me to, but that doesn't feel right. I guess none of this feels right.

"Like I said, stay vigilant. The Ravens will stop at nothing."

Then, without so much as a goodbye—not even a half-hearted wave—Norman Darby turns and cuts a stealthy path through the trees running the perimeter of the farm. Mya and I hang back, just for a minute or so, half expecting to see a sign of him emerging from the trees on the other side, but we never do.

"Come on," Mya says after a good chunk of time has passed. "The sooner we get home, the better I'll feel."

"Sure," I reply. But we both know that isn't exactly true.

Nothing is going to make us safe after learning the horrible truths we learned tonight from Norman Darby. Nothing.

We sneak down Friendly Court at twenty minutes past one o'clock.

I cover Mya while she sneaks back through the side gate and slips into the house through the back door, and then I follow.

"Good night," I tell Mya, but it's not a good night.

Morning is still a good four hours away, and I can't fathom how I'll sleep. I can't imagine how anything beyond lying here running through each and every revelation from Norman Darby will be possible.

I don't know how I could possibly feel even the slightest drop of hope that we can overcome this imbalance in the scales of justice, with all the most powerful and influential people of Raven Brooks poised to protect their fortunes no matter what.

Then, as happens a lot these days, I think of Lucy. Lucy. Good, sweet Lucy. Who just last month was annoying me like Mya and Maritza and Trinity, but now she haunts me in my daydreams. Only this time Lucy isn't crying out for help or pleading for answers or screaming at me for what we allowed to happen.

This time, I'm remembering the story about her making her dad believe in fairies. Someone mentioned it at her funeral, but it came as no surprise to me because Lucy herself had told us the story. She'd been five years old, and her dad was attempting to dissuade her from her ardent belief in the magical creatures. Lucy would not be swayed.

"What proof do you have that they *don't* exist?" she'd asked her dad.

"Sweetie, that isn't the way it works. We don't believe in something until we find a reason not to. We believe in something when we've found a reason to believe in it."

The concept had been so foreign to Lucy. Why on earth would anyone limit their possibilities that way?

Lucy's dad, ever the pragmatist, had no rebuttal for her logic. And so, from that day forward, both Lucy and her dad believed in fairies, even going so far as to build a fairy lodge in the backyard and to leave out juice and pretzels (because of course fairies love juice and pretzels).

Lucy hadn't just worn her dad down into pretending to believe. She'd actually changed his mind. She'd managed to overcome the fossilized logic of the adult brain. And it hadn't even occurred to her that she was doing the impossible.

"I owe it to Lucy," I say to myself, sometime between the gray predawn and the orange rise of the sun. "We all owe it to her."

And not just to Lucy. To everyone who has suffered for too long at the hands of a powerful few. To my parents. My grandparents. To Raven Brooks.

Raven Brooks might have been built on a conspiracy of Ravens, but they could just as easily be brought down by a murder of crows. And someone's got to do something about it.

That someone is me.

I guess it's not a bad thing I have access to the town newspaper . . .

CHAPTER 10

The next evening, Mya and I invite Enzo, Trinity, and Maritza to our house. We told them it was for board games. But it's actually to tell them what's happened in the past few hours. Enzo rubs his head like it hurts.

"You've got to be kidding me," he says, but he knows I'm not. "Please, Aaron, tell me you're kidding me. You *used* me. I could have gotten in a ton of trouble! My *dad* could have gotten into a lot of trouble. But I guess that doesn't matter to you, huh?"

"Enzo, I couldn't wait for you," I say.

"No, that's not it. You knew I wouldn't do it. The *Banner* doesn't run phony stories, and you knew that."

"Enzo, maybe you should hear him out," Trinity says, but neither she nor Maritza looks too inclined to do that. I shouldn't expect Enzo to, either.

Only Mya's on my side.

"Maybe if you explain it again," Maritza says, and instead of feeling like a complete jerk, I only feel like half of one for a second.

"Maybe you're right," I tell Enzo. It's not like the truth is going to hurt me at this point. "I knew you wouldn't be on board. But this is important, Enzo. Our plan won't work otherwise."

"*Your* plan," he says bitterly. "I don't have anything to do with it."

His words pierce me, each puncture deeper than the last.

"It's for my dad. Wouldn't you do the same for your dad?" I try to reason.

"It would never *be* my dad," he spits back.

Ah.

There it is.

I knew the town of Raven Brooks blamed my dad for, well, everything. I knew some of my teachers did, too. But I only had an inkling, a tiny, smudgy inkling, that Enzo did. And when he says that, it hangs in the air. Because I know it's what he's wanted to say to me since the day he met me, since the day I shook his hand and introduced myself as a Peterson.

I can feel the blood rise in my body, right up to my face. I bet I look red. Beet red. I think Trinity must see it, too, because she interjects.

"Could everyone just take a deep breath, please?" Trinity says, and while peacemaker is normally a comfortable role for her, she looks like she's growing tired of it. "What's done is done. The story is going to print; it's too late to change that now. So, what do we do? Aaron, you said you still need our help," she says.

I'm not ready to let Enzo off the hook for what he's said, and he doesn't look inclined to overlook what I've done, but fighting about it isn't going to help my dad.

"According to Mr. Darby—" I start, but Enzo interrupts.

"*Alleged* Mr. Darby," he says. "A real journalist would have given you more credentials than evidence that he's been stalking you."

"It was him," Mya says, a cooler head prevailing. "Mrs. Ryland confirmed it."

"Oh yes, how could I forget? You dragged our teacher into this, too," Enzo says.

"Enzo," Maritza spits, looking physically pained over the conflict. "Aaron's apologized, and besides, he and Mya are the ones taking on the majority of the risk, not us."

That isn't what Enzo's upset about, though. He's mad because he doesn't think I trusted him enough to include him.

Maybe I didn't. Maybe I've begun to feel for weeks now that no matter how much he said he was my friend, there was a growing chasm between us.

"Thanks to Mrs. Ryland," I start again, ignoring that piercing pain in my gut, "we have it on expert authority that there's a huge weather event predicted for Sunday."

"Which there isn't," Trinity says, making sure she's following.

"Exactly," Mya says. "This is all part of our plan."

"But we want the Ravens to *think* there's going to be a storm so they'll gather for a ceremony."

"Hang on. I thought Darby said that the weather events were caused by the ceremonies, not the other way around," says Maritza.

"One affects the other, I guess," I say. "They can't do anything without the weather, and once they do something, the weather gets worse. That's why the devices have weather sensors in them. And that's why the storms and the birds go crazy after they've done their ritual, or whatever it is they do."

"And that's why Mr. Darby said the balance needs to be restored," adds Mya. "The Ravens have thrown it all out of whack, the weather *and* the fortune."

"Who knows what kind of danger they'll put us all in if they keep messing with the weather," Trinity reasons.

"Not just the weather," I say. "They're taking all the good fortune, maybe even away from other people who should be getting it."

"All right," Trinity says, "so we get them to perform their ritual-thingy . . . So what? They've been doing it forever, and no one has stopped them yet."

"That's because all the powerful, rich people have been in on it," Enzo says. "Who would stop them?"

"We will," I say. "We're going to catch them in the act."

"Aren't you forgetting something?" Trinity says, dubious. "The missing device? Or rather, the missing *piece*. Why would Gordon Cleave bother being there if you have a chunk of his device?"

"Does the ritual even work if one of them is missing?" Maritza says.

"I don't know," I say, "but Cleave will be there. We're going to make sure of it."

* * *

The weather is a far cry from the apocalyptic mess my planted story in the newspaper is threatening for Sunday. It's possible I may have gone a little overboard in the description. Hopefully, Mrs. Ryland's faux explanation helps to even out the bluff. I'm sure she would have done anything to ensure I didn't come knocking on her bunker door for a rewrite.

"Good day for tacos," Maritza says, licking the adobo sauce from her finger.

"How do we even know they'll be here?" Enzo says, slurping his soda. He only had money for one taco, which he finished in two bites. He refused the one I offered him.

"Aaron's right," Trinity says, looking toward the front entrance of the Square as townspeople begin filing in, some holding placards. "The Justice for Lucy people are meeting here today to finalize the approvals for this week's rally. Now that Detective Dale is 'Officer Tapps,' he gets assigned to things like this," she says with some satisfaction.

The investigators had been right. Somehow, they'd managed to find out before Dale Tapps that his job was on the chopping block. The only way he'd managed to salvage a place on the police force was to return to his deputy days.

"And Cleave's never too far away from him," Maritza says, pushing away her paper basket and rubbing her belly. "Probably makes him feel cool to know a cop."

"Let's see how fast they all turn on each other when they get caught," Mya says, and on that, it looks like everyone can agree.

"You all know your parts?"

"Yep," says Trinity.

"Me too," says Maritza.

"Whatever," says Enzo.

"Great," I say, eyeing the entrance nervously. No sign of Tapps or Cleave yet.

"Trinity, a little help, honey?"

Trinity's mom calls to her from the front of the crowd of gatherers in the Square. Right on cue.

"I'm up," she says, taking a deep breath. "Wish me luck."

Just as she trots over to join her parents in the organizing of townspeople, I see former-Detective-now-Officer Dale lope in, frowning deeply, an expression I'm not at all accustomed to seeing on his face.

"Looks like someone got a new outfit," Mya says.

Officer Dale hikes his pants up one side at a time, looking awkward in his shiny black shoes and brimmed hat.

"New uniform, same friend," I say as Gordon Cleave files in after him, his hair mussed and growing over his ears. He long ago ditched his tie, and only seems to make half of an effort to look presentable. Definitely not the tall, smug Channel Four guy who couldn't seem to miss a single big story.

"Okay, Trinity, do your thing," I mumble.

Trinity sneaks a glance toward us, then nods.

"Here, Mom, let me take care of the signatures for you," she says, liberating her mom from the massive clipboard while half a dozen volunteers try to ask Mrs. Bales questions at once.

"What? Oh, right, thank you, Trin," her mom says, relinquishing the paperwork before turning her attention to the gatherers. "Remember, everyone. Sundays happen rain or shine. Raven Brooks is no stranger to bad weather."

Trinity approaches Officer Dale before he can be swarmed by townspeople.

"We just need your signature here and here," Trinity says, getting the administrative bit out of the way.

"That's us!" I say, hearing our cue. Mya, Enzo, Maritza, and I all slink down from the tables by the taco stand and split off, Enzo and Maritza heading toward the bathrooms, Mya and me toward the hedge that surrounds them. Only Mya and I don't crouch. We make sure Gordon Cleave can see us.

"You ready for this?" I say.

"Yeah, cuz it's such a stretch to 'act sneaky,'" she says, flicking her fingers in air quotes.

I smile. "It's the role you were born to play."

Just then, I see from the corner of my eye the glare off a familiar set of sunglasses. Cleave is watching.

"He sees us," I say, and Mya nods. "Start sneaking."

I grab Mya by the elbow and look around suspiciously, trying not to exaggerate too much.

From the side by the crowd, I see Officer Dale take the clipboard from Trinity lazily, then sign off on the demonstration permit without even bothering to read it.

"Aaron?" Mya says a little louder. "What's this big secret?"

"Shhhh!" I scold her. "Didn't you see Tapps over there?"

"Fine," she says, playing the role of the annoyed sister perfectly.

Maybe a little too perfectly.

"Oh no," I hear Trinity say from the back of the crowd. "One of the forms is missing. Hang on, maybe . . . oh, can you just come with me? It's got to be in my mom's bag over here by the bathrooms."

Officer Dale hesitates.

"I'm sorry," Trinity says with perfect sincerity. "There are probably tons of volunteers who have questions for you. I know Mrs. Tillman had some concerns about the port-a-johns, and Mr. Quinn was concerned about how the sound system might hurt his dog's ears, and—"

"No, no," I hear Officer Dale say, "I, uh, I'll go with you."

Just then, Mya and I make it to our "hiding place" by the hedge. I wait to start talking until I spy Gordon Cleave disappear around the opposite corner, then I move with Mya to the edge of the wall.

"I built a device," I say excitedly.

"You *what*?" Mya says, incredulous. "No way. You're lying."

"Oh yeah, then what do you call this?" I say, holding out an empty hand to Mya behind the wall, jutting my elbow out to finish the illusion.

"Holy cheese, Aaron, how . . . how is this even possible?"

"That dummy Cleave didn't even realize he dropped a piece of it when he stole it," I say, snickering.

"Grandma and Grandpa's notes made it easy after that," I say.

"But . . . I mean, do you even know what it does?" Mya asks.

"Guess we're about to find out!" I say. "I just need to put some finishing touches on it. I'll take it for a test run on Sunday while everyone's at the Justice for Lucy thing. Mom and Dad will be gone for a couple of hours at least."

"You'd better hide that thing when you're done tinkering with it," she says.

We wait for a surge of noise from the nearby crowd to die down until I say my last part.

"I'll just bury it under all that junk on Dad's desk sometime tomorrow."

"Are you nuts?" Mya says.

"Well, I can't exactly hide it in my room; he and Mom have been snooping all over ever since we got caught sneaking out the other night. The last place he'll think to look is in his own mess."

"Just tell me when you're going to test it out," she says. "I don't want to miss this."

Then I hear Trinity's perfectly timed arrival.

"I think my mom left her bag just around the corner here," she says.

"Shhh, someone's coming!" Mya hisses, and we bolt from our places near the hedges and disappear through the back exit of the Square.

"Do you think it worked?" she says, breathless as we slow to a walk and make our way back toward the house, our designated meeting spot.

"Guess we'll have to wait and see," I say. "It's up to Enzo and Maritza now."

* * *

"It worked," Trinity says excitedly from the floor of my bedroom.

"Totally worked," agrees Maritza.

"Let's just see if they take the bait before we get excited," Enzo says, but even he can't hide his giddiness. Scheming is in his blood, just like the rest of us—it's pointless to deny it.

"You should have heard him," Maritza says. "He was like a double agent, all 'Did you hear that, Maritza? We've got to get our hands on that device before Sunday! I think we're due for a little good luck,' blah blah blah."

Trinity laughs. "I wish I could have heard it. I was too busy coaxing Mrs. Tillman away so Tapps could hear the rest of your conversation."

Then Trinity smirks. "I made sure she got to corner him for lots and lots of port-a-john questions later on, though."

"Nice," I say.

"Okay, so Cleave and Tapps think we have a fully functioning device," says Mya.

"And they think we're going to steal it away from your house Sunday morning when we come to pick you up for the rally," Maritza says.

"Which means if they're going to try to steal it from the base-ment, they're going to have to try to do it tomorrow night or risk losing it again."

"Uh, about that 'device,' Enzo says, the next step in the plan suddenly taking on new urgency. "Isn't there that small detail about you not actually having a fully working device?"

But I've already thought of that.

From underneath my mattress, I withdraw my greatest

Fake-Out 3000

Maker: Aaron Peterson

Never get caught!

Not yet tested

creation yet: The Fake-Out 3000 (patent pending).

"Whoa," Enzo says, finally impressed.

"That . . . that looks so real," Maritza breathes.

"How did you do that?" says Trinity.

"*When* did you do that?" Mya says.

I shrug, trying hard to be modest, but man, this decoy is a thing of beauty.

"I couldn't really sleep last night," I say. "And the garden shed out back has a bunch of old rusty scraps I didn't even know were there before."

Enzo takes it gently from my hand. "It's even heavy like the real thing!"

"Yeah, that's about fifteen melted-down marbles," I say.

Mya squints closer at the decoy device. She's eyeing the crescent with its purple jewel.

"You used the real piece? Are you nuts?"

"I had to," I say. "It would have been impossible to replicate otherwise."

I was an idiot to think she wouldn't notice, but I was still hoping to dodge this question.

"You realize you're giving Cleave back the one thing keeping him from becoming a Raven again. Then he gets to keep on ruining our lives," Mya says, agog that she even has to tell me.

"The rest of the device is completely fake," I remind her. "By the time he realizes the only real part is the crescent with the jewel, we'll have caught them in the act."

Mya still looks uncomfortable until Trinity speaks up. "I mean, he probably doesn't even know how to put the device back together anyway, even once he does get his hands on the missing piece."

"It'll all be worth it in the end," I say, and I'm sure of at least that much. "It's for Dad."

Maybe, just maybe, things are starting to go back to the way they were, because not even the mention of my dad manages to cast a shadow over the room.

Maybe these last couple of months have just been a blip—one of those bumps in the road grown-ups are always talking about when they have to deal with hard stuff.

"I have to pee," Maritza says, breaking my meditation.

"Thanks for sharing," Enzo smirks.

Maritza scoots out and down the hallway. I think nothing of it until I hear a voice.

"Ah, hello, young friend!" I hear my dad's voice boom.

I'm not gonna lie; I'm about as stunned as everyone else in my room looks. I'm pretty sure that's the first time I've heard my dad's voice in the daytime for . . . how long has it been?

Dad? Mya mouths to me, and I nod because what else is there to do? Everything about this is absurd.

"Um . . . hi, Mr. Peterson," Maritza's voice answers, so tiny it doesn't even sound like her.

Then we hear Maritza's footsteps sneak past him. She's in the clear.

I smooth down the hairs on my arm that seem to have jutted up. *Other kids don't have to worry about their dad like I do,* I remind myself. *For anyone else's family, that interaction would have been totally normal.*

"Okay, so the plan for tomorrow," Trinity says, getting us back on track. "We'll need you and at least one other person in the tunnels, ready to catch the action on film."

"And I'll need to be at the Justice for Lucy rally to report for the *Banner*," says Enzo.

"Which is perfect because you'll be able to record the town's reaction when the whole Raven conspiracy blows up."

Enzo sits up a little bit taller. I can tell he's proud. After all, his job is important.

I'm so engrossed in the plans, I barely see Maritza walk back through my bedroom door. Then I do a double take. *Maritza?*

She's pale—no, gray. She's the color of old bones I've seen on skeletons behind glass panels. She doesn't sit down.

She bends at her waist and leans toward Enzo's ear.

"Can we go?" she says quietly, just like she spoke in the hallway.

"Yeah, in a sec. We're just working out the details for tomorrow."

"Now," she says, a little more insistently.

"Are you okay?" Mya asks, exchanging a concerned look with Trinity.

But when Mya goes to touch her friend's hand, Maritza shrinks back so fast, she almost falls over.

"Whoa, what happened in there?" Enzo says, having the same thought I did. "Was it the tacos? Wouldn't be the first story I heard about tacos."

"Enzo, *please!*" she says, and this time she's so urgent, I'm starting to worry, too. "I need to leave."

"Um . . . okay," Enzo replies, clearly as confused as the rest of us. He looks at me and shrugs.

"It's okay, I think we've got it mostly worked out. I'll call you to let you know how tomorrow night goes," I say. After all, if Maritza really is sick from the tacos, I know from experience that she *definitely* doesn't want to be at her friends' house.

"Cool," he says, and before he can even get the "—ool" out, Maritza has left the room. Seconds later, the front door swings open and shut.

"What was that all about?" Trinity says.

Mya looks at us, bewildered.

I shake my head. "Taco fever. It's gotten us all at some point," I say.

* * *

In the morning, Mom makes us chocolate chip muffins. They're nobody's favorite but we're hardly complaining. I shovel them into my mouth like my life depends on it.

"What on earth?" Mom says, watching as some of the crumbs dangle from my chin.

"I don't know, they're just so good," I say.

For the first time in I can't remember how long, it doesn't feel like the food in my stomach is competing for space beside the lead brick that formed the minute we left Germany.

I'm not the only one, either. Dad's at the table, too, which

149

changes everything so drastically, it's like he's been away for a decade. And he isn't just at the table. He's really *here*.

"Diane, sit, eat your breakfast. You deserve a muffin, too," he says jovially. He's looking out for her the way he used to. If I didn't know better, I'd have thought we time-traveled back a few months.

"Okay, I'm not going to ask what's happening here, because I'm sure I won't understand," Mom says, airing what we're all thinking, "but . . . who are you people and what have you done with my family?"

Dad laughs harder than is called for, but it's so good to hear him laugh, it doesn't bother me in the least. Mya and I look at each other, wide-eyed and giddy. It's like the mood is contagious, and we all can't wait to get sick.

Apparently, Dad even took a little leisure time to do the crossword. I can see the Puzzles page of the *Banner* jammed into his back pocket when he stands to get more food. Which is weird because I didn't do a crossword for today's paper. I didn't see a need for it after meeting with Norman Darby.

I squint at the visible part of the paper folded over my dad's waistband. I can't see the telltale rows and columns that usually take up the entire top left quadrant of the page. Instead, I see a series of what look to be letters, symbols, and maybe even a few backward letters. Scribbles in red ink bunch together along the margins.

Dad turns before I have a chance to see much more.

"I have news," Dad says, and this morning just keeps getting weirder because when's the last time he's had news . . . news that he'd want to share at the dining table, anyway?

"Ted, if you're about to say we're moving again, I swear—"

"The Germans dropped their investigation."

We all drop our muffins at the same time.

"What?" Mom says. She doesn't look excited. She looks suspicious. I understand—happiness is hard to trust these days.

"They just *dropped* it? All of it? Flew back home to Germany?"

"Just like that," Dad says, holding up his hands and wiggling his fingers. Poof, gone. Like it never happened.

"How . . . *how*?"

All I can do is watch the spectacle. It's so beautiful, and yet . . . there's something I just can't place. Like it's not over. How can such a big problem float away, just like that? Just like how Dad said?

Whatever it is, it's the same dizziness my mom is struggling with, and to a lesser extent, Mya. She hasn't touched her muffin since dropping it back on her plate, either.

"Allegedly, once the German authorities dug in, they realized there was nothing to find," Dad says, almost like he's as surprised as the investigators must have been.

"So, they didn't get what they were looking for," Mya says.

"Wow," Mom says after a while.

"Wow is right," Dad replies. "In fact, wow is

cause for celebration!" He moves so suddenly, he startles Mom, who jerks back reflexively. Then he plants a giant kiss on her cheek and Dad turns his entire body to face my mom.

Mom and I finally find each other across the table, and I'm not sure if it's real or if she's slapping a smile on just for me, but she lets out a small laugh and shakes her head, turning to look at my dad as he returns to the table.

"Ted, this is just such a *relief*," she says, tasting the word like she's not sure it's real.

Dad sets his plate down, sits in his chair, and turns his entire body to face my mom.

"And that's not all."

"I'm not sure I can take much more," says Mom, but Dad isn't stopping.

"That lawyer of yours might have just found a loophole in the property tax law."

I drop my muffin. Again.

"He called last night all excited," Dad rushes ahead. "He was sitting in Gary's Garlic Grotto and overheard some bank bigwig—Harold something-or-other—blathering about how easy it would be for people to keep their houses if they only knew about this teeny, tiny loophole in the tax code."

I want to be excited. This means we don't lose the house. But I heard absolutely nothing after "garlic grotto," and judging by the pallor of Mya's face, that's where she stopped listening, too.

Garlic. The man with the garlic breath in the tunnels. Another Raven.

"Diane," Dad says, pulling her small hand into his giant one. "This is the beginning of a turn in our luck."

Luck?

Dad barks a full, deep laugh. "Things are going to change for us, Diane."

He turns to Mya and me.

"For all of us."

But no matter how much I want to bask in the snowfall of words Dad covered us in, one of those words keeps melting that delicate snow away. One of them swirls around my head like the worst weather of the season.

Why did he have to say "luck"?

CHAPTER 11

Later that day, it's like breakfast never happened. By lunchtime, Dad acts like he's been a man possessed. Mom seems as baffled as Mya and me.

"Penknife . . . Honey? The penknife. Have you seen it?" Dad bellows from the top of the basement stairs.

"The what?" Mom says.

Dad blows past her and rummages through one kitchen drawer after another, first the junk drawer, then every single place a penknife would absolutely not be.

"Ted, it's not going to be with the pastry cutter," Mom replies.

He whips around to find Mya and me standing in the living room, where we search for any trace of the Dad from the morning.

"You kids know better than to play with it," he says, accusing us of stealing a knife I haven't laid eyes on in at least five years. I can't even be sure it left Germany with us.

"Never mind, I'll just have to use something else," he says, whipping a paring knife from the block on the counter.

"Not the good ones," Mom says, frowning.

"Take the rusty one at least."

He takes the knife back in his

hand. Then he cuts a quick path to the hallway. He stops about six feet away from Mya and me.

"I'll be in my office," he says coolly. "Important things going on. Under no circumstances are you—or *anyone*—to disturb me. Got it?"

Mya and I nod. Then he's gone, the dust he's kicked up still swirling in the air.

I lean toward Mya. "How long do you suppose he'll be down there?" I ask. After all, we have plans—plans that hinge upon accessing his office.

She shakes her head. "He'll have to leave at some point. We'll just keep an eye out."

"We need at least five minutes to get down there, plant the decoy, and leave before he knows we were there."

Mya tries to calm me. "Five minutes. The man has to go to the bathroom sometime. Maybe we should try feeding him some of Maritza's tacos. That would do the trick." Mya laughs, but I can tell she hasn't forgotten the weird way that Maritza and Enzo left last night.

But apparently, Dad *doesn't* need to use the bathroom. Or if he does, he only needs to go during the exact moment I'm upstairs blowing my nose, or Mya is stuck in the kitchen helping Mom clean out the spice drawer, or we get a telemarketer calling about insuring our award-winning show dogs (either an elaborate prank by someone in Raven Brooks or a really hilarious business model).

"We're never going to get a chance to plant that device," Mya tells me through gritted teeth in the midafternoon.

"It's only three o'clock," I say.

The problem, though, is that then it's only four o'clock, then five. Then five thirty. We're running out of hours in the day.

"What's going on with you two?"

"Your hovering is making me more nervous than your dad and his . . . whatever this latest thing is," Mom says, waving her arms like we're all flies buzzing around her head. "Don't you kids go outside and play anymore? They really need to teach sports in school again . . ."

All of a sudden, the phone's ring slices straight through our nerves.

Then, like a charging bull, Dad comes thundering up the basement stairs, hollering with every bounding step.

"Do *not* answer the phone," he barks.

What? What's the worst it could be—someone calling about insuring my award-winning *armadillo* now? I keep reaching because it's instinct, the ringing of the phone is buzzing all around us. But then Dad crashes through the hall and lunges into the living room, shouldering me with the skill of a linebacker. He tackles me to the floor.

"Ted! Ted!" Mom screams. The phone stops ringing.

More than anything I'm just . . . stunned. Dad gets up and looks like he's about to apologize, but then I see a cog in his head turn. He's got more pressing questions.

"How many rings was that?" he says suddenly.

We all stare at him, jaws slack.

"How many rings?"

"Six! It was six!" Mya says.

Dad stares at the phone like it's about to talk to him, even though he hasn't even lifted the receiver.

With the echo of the ring lingering in the stunned silence of the house, a slow smile spreads over Dad's face.

"He got it," he says, then laughs hysterically. "He got the message."

He laughs for a full minute. Actual tears leak from his crinkled eyes. I massage my elbow. What is going *on*?

Dad doesn't seem to notice that we've all been gawking at him. He doesn't even seem to notice we're here. Instead, he snaps his fingers, takes a step toward the basement, does a little honest-to-bagels skip, and descends the stairs once again, the door thudding shut behind him.

Mya blinks. Then she looks at her watch.

"Six o'clock. We're running out of time."

By nine o'clock that night, Mya is in a full-blown panic, leaving me to be the collected one, which is a little terrifying.

"Look, all we need is five minutes. Worst-case scenario, one of us can just . . . I don't know, flush him out of there somehow."

"By what, running a fire drill? This isn't school, Aaron."

I can tell Mya's stressed so I don't push it. I'm stressed, too. Then we hear a sharp tap on the door to my room. It's Mom.

"I'm going to bed," she says, then squints at us.

"You should get to bed early, too. Tomorrow's going to be . . ."

Mya's face stiffens, but I know that look. She's hardening the outside because she's crumbling on the inside.

The Justice for Lucy town assembly has been one heavy,

looming cloud among many. Mya's been so stoic through it all, but nobody's strong enough to see the light through a cloud that thick.

"We'll go to bed soon," Mya says to Mom, and Mom steps into the room to give us each a quick but thorough squeeze before padding off to her room.

Now, just Dad.

By eleven o'clock, Mya is despondent.

"It's over," she groans.

"It's not over."

"Aaron, I don't know when you became the family optimist, but I have to tell you, it's getting kind of annoying."

And then, a miracle. The basement door creaks open, the sound of Dad's footsteps landing on the stairs, the opening sigh and closing whoosh of the bedroom door. By half past eleven, Dad is sawing logs beside a fast-asleep Mom.

We creep downstairs, the decoy device forming a sweaty pool in the center of my palm. We're too skittish to even turn on the light to the basement stairs, so we grope our way down instead, counting the steps to the basement floor.

Down the long, crooked hallway to Dad's office, we don't dare breathe a word. For all we know, Gordon Cleave is already at the mouth of the tunnel, not knowing there would be any reason to doubt the device would be there.

Surely, eleven thirty would be too early in the night for him to risk sneaking into the office.

I try telling that to my racing heart, but it doesn't want to listen.

Mya must be having similar thoughts because she doesn't breathe a word, either. Instead, she quietly pushes the office door open, letting the door swing to a full stop, then waiting in the doorway, lingering in the shadow of the hall. Better to be cautious, I'd bet.

After a minute of complete silence, we're convinced that no one is waiting to spring from the dark corners of the office, and Mya clicks on Dad's desk lamp, waving me over after pulling up a pile of scribbled notes. Tucked under the lamp is the same folded paper Dad had sticking out of his pocket.

The red scribbles I'd spotted from a distance don't make much more sense close-up. I make out "real" and "night" and maybe "b-a-l." The rest is a jumble of scribbles.

Mya nudges my shoulder, and I see that she's holding up a stack of papers on Dad's desk. What's under them, however, is something neither one of us expected to find.

"Wait . . . what?" I say, forgetting to keep quiet.

Apparently, Mya forgets, too. "Is that what I think it is?" she says. It looks to be the very same device that went missing from this office the first time Gordon Cleave snuck in and stole it.

"Holy cheese . . . Mya, Dad did it. He actually made a new device."

Mya picks the object up and examines it under the light of the desk lamp.

"This fake is even better than yours!" she marvels.

Mya sets it carefully in my palm, and I wish I

could argue, but she's right. Dad's decoy is a dead ringer for the real thing. He's even managed to make the metal look weathered and tarnished, age-worn like the ancient relic Mr. Darby claimed it is.

"This is great!" Mya says suddenly. "Now we don't have to turn over the actual piece from your decoy. We can use this!"

I hadn't considered that. She's not wrong. This does seem like the perfect solution to protecting the actual device piece.

Except one thing. One very, VERY important thing.

"We don't even know why Dad made this replica, though."

"Maybe he's just trying to understand whatever he found in Grandma and Grandpa's diagrams. You know, like building a model car," she hisses. "This is a miracle!"

"The tide is turning," I mutter, then look at Mya. "That's what he said earlier. That our luck is finally turning around."

Mya shrugs. "Maybe it's finally our turn to catch a break."

"Okay . . . okay," I say, thinking as fast as I can. "The plan doesn't change. We just leave Dad's decoy where it is. I'll take mine apart later."

"And Cleave never gets his hands on the missing piece," Mya confirms.

The plan is a solid one.

Mya lets out a huge breath. "That was close. Can you imagine if we hadn't come down here and found this? Cleave would've gotten it."

"Crisis averted," I reply. "Let's just get out of here before he comes."

We skid out of the basement as fast as we can. Then we reach the top of the stairs and step into the living room . . . where my heart plummets, my hands feel clammy.

Because there, plain as day, decked out in robe and slippers, arms crossed over his expansive chest, is . . . Dad.

And he heard us.

"I don't need to ask where you were," he says, his voice frighteningly quiet.

"What I *would* like to know," he says slowly, "is *why* you were there."

Mya feels too far away. I want to step backward to shield her better, but I'm afraid to move.

"And what is it you're hiding behind your back."

"It's my fault," I say before Mya can take the fall.

Dad turns his gaze to me. "Oh, I have no doubt of that."

Then his stare refocuses on Mya. "But that doesn't answer my question."

When Mya doesn't move—maybe *can't* move—I turn and retrieve the device from behind her and hold it out to Dad, steadying my hands as much as I can.

Dad stares at the device for so long, I can't figure out what's going on in his head.

Until he speaks.

"Where did you get this?" he says slowly, carefully, yet enough to make me want to vomit, here and now.

"I . . . I made it," I say. I can't possibly get myself into *more* trouble by telling the truth, can I?

Dad stares tiny pinholes into me. I picture moonlit beams emanating from every puncture point on my body.

"You *made* it?"

I nod. He doesn't believe me.

He studies the device long enough for me to run through every possible punishment he might lay upon me. It's boarding school for sure. Maybe the guillotine. Or maybe he'll just feed me to a hungry pack of llamas and be done with it.

Maybe I'll be sent to volunteer at Mrs. Tillman's grocery.

I shudder hard enough to creak the floorboards.

Finally, Dad speaks.

"You have no idea what you almost did," he says so quietly, it's almost impossible to hear him. What I can't miss, though, is the way he's doing the same thing with his hands that I'm doing with mine—trying to keep them from trembling.

Then the strangest thing of all happens. He doesn't ask us anything else. He doesn't even yell at us. It's almost like he doesn't want to know any more than he already does.

"Whatever you thought you were doing . . ." he says, his eyes never leaving the device in his hand. "Don't ever do it again."

Dad doesn't go into detail about whatever "it" is, and we don't ask him to because when I make a move for the stairs, Dad doesn't stop me. Mya follows quickly behind, and when we meet in front of our bedroom doors, Mya whips around to face me.

"He knows. He knows."

"I don't know what he knows," I say. "All I know is he didn't say the word 'grounded.'"

"It means we don't have the actual device anymore," Mya says, her forehead crinkled. "Or the real piece anyway."

"Yeah, but Dad does. So, it's still in safe hands."

"But he doesn't know it's real! What if he loses it? What if he destroys it? What if—?"

"We'll work on that part later. Right now, at least we know that the one in the office is the decoy. Worst-case scenario, Gordon Cleave will be stealing a fake tonight. And that's exactly what we want."

Mya nods, but she's unconvinced, and I can't say I feel much better. After tonight, it's going to be way harder to find the device and sneak it away from Dad before any more damage can be done. It'll probably be under lock and key.

Still, one problem at a time. Problem numero uno, we expose the Ravens. Then, after their society crumbles, we'll have help rounding up the devices and figuring out what to do with them.

Easy-peasy, right?

Easy-peasy.

* * *

I'm fast asleep when the sound of the front door wakes me. I'm about to go into the hall to check it out when I hear footsteps echoing outside on the sidewalk below. From my window, I see Dad.

I watch him for as long as I can before he disappears out of sight midway down Friendly Court. *What?* I think to myself. *What's going on?*

I sneak into Mya's room and nudge her a little too hard, yanking her from sleep.

"What's wrong? What happened?" she says, eyes wide, both hands gripping my wrist.

"Dad just left."

"What do you mean 'left'?"

"Like walked out the door and went for a stroll in the middle of the night," I say.

"We should follow him," Mya says, subscribing to the this-is-totally-normal logic.

I shake my head. "He's too far ahead. There's no way we'd be able to catch him unless you have a rocket or something."

Mya's grip tightens again. "We should check the basement. We have to know if Cleave took the bait."

Of course. Mya's totally right. That's exactly what we have to do. Even if we're risking certain doom.

This time, we get smarter. Mya stands guard at the top of the basement steps as I fly down the stairs, stumbling and catching myself just before I trip over the last step.

Dad's office is once again quiet and dark, and again, I'm struck by the luck necessary for the plan to work. Each time I come down here, I run the risk of catching Cleave in the act, and then the whole thing crumbles.

I switch on the lamp and am relieved to find the room empty.

Then, wasting no time at all, I go straight to the stack of papers where Mya and I left Dad's decoy in place.

Only it's gone.

I exhale.

"Cleave stole it," I mutter to myself.

I check the stack once, then twice. I check it a third time to be absolutely certain. No device.

What's more, when I chance a peek at the passage door, I

discover the rug in front of it has been moved ever so slightly. The corner closest to the passage door has been folded over, as though someone accidentally nudged it with their toe. I'm sure the rug wasn't like that earlier in the night when Mya and I were down here.

Someone opened that passage door.

"Aaron!"

I hear Mya's panicked voice float down the stairs and through the hallway to the office.

Someone's coming.

I race back down the hall and up the steps two at a time, meeting her at the basement door.

"It's Dad! He's halfway down the street, or he was when I called you, so—"

"So let's get the heck out of here," I say, and we book it back up the stairs just in time to hear the front door carefully open and click closed.

When we're at the top of the stairs, Mya glares at me. I know the question written all over her face. *Was it there?*

I shake my head no.

For the first time today, Mya's body seems to shrink down to its normal size, like she's allowed herself to deflate, be a normal kid again. And for the first time in months, I realize I'm jealous. Jealous of Mya. Because I can't relax. I can't concentrate. Not until I find out what Dad was doing up this late.

CHAPTER 12

The following morning feels like the final curve of a full circle.

Mom pops her head into my room and tells me it's time to wake up. Only this time, it isn't Lucy's funeral I'm dreading—it's her *rally*. And it isn't only Lucy who deserves justice.

It's an entire town—an entire town of crows.

One look at the dark crescents cupping Mya's eyes tells me she got about as much sleep as I did.

Before we even have a chance to say good morning to each other, I hear Mom on the phone, fervently agreeing with someone.

"I know, I know. Honestly, they should probably just postpone the whole thing. I can't imagine it's safe for us all to be out there in that weather."

I peer out the front window from the landing of the stairs. It's a little overcast maybe, but nothing dire.

As though divining my thoughts, Mom says into the phone, "They say it's going to pick up by later this morning. By midafternoon . . . I don't even want to think about it."

Mya catches my attention. "If the storm is going to be that big, the Ravens will definitely try a ritual," she says.

I agree, but that doesn't exactly make me feel better. "Which means if they have a chance to complete it, they could make a bad storm a hundred times worse."

I don't mention the very real possibility that one more ritual could doom our family for good.

"Then we don't let them finish," says Mya.

It's hard not to feel like there are a million ways the plan could go wrong today.

"I know you're right. Can you imagine the uproar if you were to cancel?"

Good. Then the plan is still on. Good.

The second Mom hangs up the phone, it rings again.

"It's like a switchboard in here this morning," she mutters, then chirps another hello into the receiver.

"Oh, hi, Enzo," she says warmly. "Mhmm, I know, I was just speaking with Trinity's mother about that. According to her, the rally is still on. Yes, exactly. Did you want to speak with Aaron?"

Mom extends the phone to me a second later, and I have to say, it feels pretty great knowing that he *did* want to speak with me.

That feeling fades the second I hear his voice, though.

"Did you put another message on the Puzzle page for Darby?"

This isn't friend Enzo. This is Junior Reporter Enzo. And he sounds very, very ready to believe I went behind his back. Again.

"What? No. Of course not. Why?"

"Have you seen the paper yet?" he says.

"Hang on."

I scan the kitchen and living room before opening the door and finding the paper still bundled on the front step.

I return to the phone and spread the Puzzles page before me.

"Now you've got *me* looking for hidden messages," Enzo grumbles.

It's another cipher, like the one I spotted in yesterday's paper.

"It's not a crossword," I say, surprised that I feel a little betrayed. It's not like I ever really liked being the Puzzles editor, but two different puzzles I had nothing to do with is a pretty clear indication that I've been replaced.

"Then you didn't have anything to do with it?" he says.

"How could I? I don't even know what *it* is!"

"It's a code."

"Okay, yes. I know that much, but who could possibly decode this?"

I envision my dad's red scrawls on yesterday's paper. My dad, that's who.

"It says 'device is safe. PM.'"

"Hold on. You decoded it?"

I can almost hear Enzo shrugging. "I'm good at codes."

"That's great! Did you solve yesterday's, too?"

"That was a cipher," Enzo says like I'm dumb.

"Is that a no?"

"Hey, look," Enzo says defensively. "Ciphers are way harder. Every individual letter is replaced. Codes replace whole words. Can we please get back to the message?"

Right. The message.

"We already know what the device is," Enzo says. "But who's PM?"

We exchange silence for a moment, and then it hits me.

"Puzzle Master."

More silence as we consider what that means.

"Hold on," Enzo says. "Norman Darby has the device? The *real* missing piece?"

I shake my head, then remember that Enzo can't see me. "That's not possible."

"Right, because you and Mya have it. Right?"

Nope.

"My dad caught us coming out of his office with it last night," I say.

"What?" Enzo nearly barks.

"That doesn't matter," I try to reassure him. Or maybe I'm trying to reassure myself. All the commotion on the phone has drawn Mom's attention, and I laugh to try to make it sound like we're just having a totally normal, lighthearted chat.

Mom looks unconvinced, so I bring the corded phone around the corner into the living room instead, dropping my voice. I'm met by another set of prying eyes, but it's only Mya, and she might as well hear all of this now so I don't have to repeat myself.

"Look, long story, but my dad made his own decoy and he took ours away. We can get it back from him after—"

"Right, after the Ravens are exposed," Enzo says, sounding only slightly reassured. He doesn't trust the device in my dad's hands much more than he trusts it in the hands of some of the most crooked people in town. Nice.

"Right," I say.

"Right," he says.

I don't get it. I thought Enzo and I were back to . . . us. What changed between yesterday and today?

"I'll see you at the rally for Stage Two of the plan?" I say.

"Yup."

Enzo hangs up without another word.

"Norman Darby has the missing piece?" Mya whispers, pulling me farther out of earshot from Mom.

"I mean . . . maybe? I don't know. Now I'm really confused."

Then Mya's eyes go wide. "It must have been last night, when Dad left."

I consider this. "No way. How would he even know who Norman Darby is?"

Mya shakes her head slowly. "No idea. But I mean . . . I guess even if Mr. Darby does have it . . . that isn't a bad thing, either, right?"

"Yeah," I say. "And that's if it's even true. We don't know what that code really says," I say. "Enzo could have gotten it wrong."

"What's up with him?" Mya says, and I'm only half-glad that she notices it, too. On one hand, I'm not imagining it. On the other hand . . . I'm not imagining it.

"I don't know," I say, trying to act casual about it, "but we'd better get ready for Stage Two."

* * *

We thought we were leaving early for the rally, but when we arrive at the Golden Apple Amusement Park, the amphitheater is packed.

"Is it just me, or do you think this location is a bit, uh, insensitive?" Mya whispers to me as we lag behind Mom and Dad.

"I'm not sure any other place could hold this many people," I say.

Mya's right, though. It's a weird locale. I spot the unmistakable arc of the Rotten Core's apex looming in the summer storm fog at the back of the park.

"It'll be over soon," I say, and Mya looks back up at me, her eyes glassy. She blinks her tears away, and I can see her refocusing on the mission at hand.

The minute we set foot on the Golden Apple Amusement Park grounds, we can hear the nagging voice of Mayor Tavish echoing on the electric air.

"If we could please take our seats! I think we're all eager to get through this before the storm lands."

He's standing on the amphitheater stage, looking decidedly less grand (and penguin-like) than the last time he was in public. His collared shirt is partially untucked; his tie is loose and askew around his neck. His hair might have been combed at some point, but the storm winds have loosened his part, and he looks almost disoriented up there behind a microphone that stands a little too high for him.

He looks to the side of the stage anxiously, but instead of receiving any comfort, a uniformed Officer Tapps and a disheveled Gordon Cleave seem just as worried.

If the rally doesn't end soon, they won't be able to perform the ceremony during the storm.

"People, please!" Mayor Tavish shouts into the microphone. "If we could begin expediently!"

"He's blowing us off again!" an angry voice shouts.

"Is anyone surprised?" says someone else, and the question is met with another chorus of agreement.

From the back of the crowd, two townspeople wheel a large sort of easel to the front of the amphitheater, a picture of Lucy's kind face shining through her frame of black hair. I feel an unexpected sob catch in my throat. I can only imagine what Mya must be feeling.

To my surprise, another easel makes its way to the front from the opposite side. This one's of Ike Gershowitz. It seems to be a slightly more candid shot. He's wearing a cone-shaped party hat and holding a paper plate piled high with birthday cake. His smile covers his entire face. I imagine him as the guest everyone looked forward to seeing. He'd make anyone feel like a friend. He was the only person I ever heard my dad refer to that way. I recall the night he walked me home from the forest, stern with warning but with the protectiveness of a parent. I remember the way he covered for me. He never told my dad where it was he found me.

Ike Gershowitz was good. Even Norman Darby trusted him.

Remembering Norman Darby makes me think of Enzo, and I realize I need to find him. Fortunately for me, Enzo remembered first. As though sensing I needed him, Enzo is making his way toward me. When he reaches me, he doesn't even bother saying hello.

"They look nervous," he says, looking toward Mayor Tavish and his cohorts.

"Of course they're nervous," I say, not meaning for it to come out as defensively as it does.

Enzo looks nervous, too. I guess that's better than looking angry at me. Then he asks something that makes me think he's nervous about more than I am.

"Where's your dad?"

"My dad? Uh, I dunno. Around somewhere, I guess."

"You guess?" he says, and he almost sounds a little panicky. I guess the whole Norman-Darby-might-have-the-device thing is freaking him out a little more than I realized.

"Hey, you know if Darby has the missing piece, that's probably for the best."

"Huh?" he says, genuinely confused.

That makes two of us.

"Just . . . tell me when your dad comes back, okay?" says Enzo.

"Um, okay," I say, wanting to ask more, but suddenly, Mya's poking me and pointing toward one of the sad, abandoned snack stands to the side and behind the amphitheater.

"What's he doing?" Mya says, seeing Cleave before I do.

"I think the word they'd use if it were us instead of them is 'loitering,'" I say.

"Well, if he's loitering, so is Officer Tapps," Enzo says.

Sure enough, former detective Dale has positioned himself

between Mayor Tavish onstage and Gordon Cleave. All three are alternating between watching the sky and watching their watches. Gordon Cleave is pacing the length of the snack stand, up and down and up again, fists balling and loosening as he fails to relax himself.

"They're definitely getting antsy," I say.

"What good is catching the Ravens in the act if the Ravens aren't even there to take the fall?"

"Speaking of that—" I start.

"Trinity and Mya are already in position in the tunnels," Enzo says, his entire body tensed.

We watch as Mrs. Bales, Trinity's mom, takes the stage before Mayor Tavish invites her up, but he seems relieved to turn the microphone over to her.

"Thank you all for coming this afternoon. And on behalf of the volunteers of Justice for Lucy, I'd like to extend a special thanks to Raven Brooks leadership for their willingness to hear the people's concerns about the transparency of the investigations into both Lucy Yi's death as well as another lost friend, Ike Gershowitz."

The crowd gives applause to said Raven Brooks leadership.

"I'd now like to turn it over to Brenda Yi."

This time, the applause fills the amphitheater.

Mrs. Yi takes her place behind the microphone, seemingly unaware of the applause. She is as stoic as ever, pressed and neat even under the brewing storm.

"We're here today because tragedy has struck our town not once, but twice," Mrs. Yi says.

She pauses to collect herself, and my heart squeezes over a beat as I see her struggle not to cry. "While these two tragedies happened under vastly different circumstances, they are connected by a common issue."

The crowd rumbles agreement. They know what's coming.

"That is the issue of *accountability*. That is the issue of *transparency*," Mrs. Yi says, her voice growing louder. "That is the issue of *honesty*!"

The crowd rushes to applaud.

"When I've asked for information into my daughter's death," she says, her voice breaking over the word "death," "I've been met with vague answers, soft promises, and reassurances that 'we're on it,'" she adds, making no effort to hide the long glance she slides toward Officer Tapps.

Only now do I see that Officer Keith is there as well, looking as uncomfortable as ever in his uniform, but at least he seems to be paying attention to Mrs. Yi. Officer Tapps, Gordon Cleave, and Mayor Tavish are shooting one another anxious looks and are clearly unconcerned with what's happening onstage.

"And how about Ike?" someone from the crowd hollers.

The townspeople answer with hollers of "Who is investigating?" and "Are we even safe?" and "There could be a murderer out there!"

The storm seems to join in the outrage, sending a piece of debris away from the crowd.

"Indeed, Ike Gershowitz's death is cause for great concern," Mrs. Yi says, and the townspeople erupt in applause.

Finally taking notice of the rambunctious crowd, Mayor

Tavish tears himself away from Officer Tapps and Gordon Cleave to tend to his own microphone.

"If we could all make an effort to remain civil, please!" he says, sounding annoyed.

"*You're* telling *us* to put in more effort?" yells a voice from the amphitheater. More shouts of agreement.

"This storm is going to break any second," Mya says over the din, and as much as none of us wants Justice for Lucy to be cut short, the longer this goes on, the less likely we are to catch the Ravens and see true justice—for *everybody*.

"Where's *your* effort, Tavish?" someone yells.

"What're the police doing?"

"Where's the press coverage? Frankly, I'm surprised this hasn't been picked up national—no, internationally!—yet."

"People, *please*!" Mayor Tavish pleads.

Mrs. Yi is still onstage, but she looks like she's actually gone somewhere else. She stares into the middle distance as the world around her falls apart. She looks kind of like the only person who might deserve to make it through the storm.

The rumble of thunder ripples through the air, and apparently, that's what it takes to send Officer Tapps into action. He breaks away from Gordon Cleave and yanks Mayor Tavish to the edge of the stage, but not completely out of earshot of the microphone—especially for anybody interested in listening.

Like Mya, Enzo, and me.

"End it now, Marvin," Officer Tapps growls.

"Are you nuts? Look at these people. They'll go ballistic!"

"Would you quit thinking about your next election and

176

remember your *real* allegiance?" Officer Tapps says, and I don't think I've ever heard him sound more threatening. Seriously. Is nobody else hearing this? But as I glance around the rest of the amphitheater—no. Nobody else is hearing this. They're far too entrenched in their own anger to hear anything else.

"Fine," Officer Tapps says after another refusal from Mayor Tavish. "Gordon and I will go without you."

"You'll throw off the balance! You morons, you'll ruin it all!" Mayor Tavish calls, and maybe it's because he is yelling this time, or maybe it's because he leans a little too close to the microphone, but the crowd finally hears.

They weren't loud before. They weren't even close to loud. They were like a bunch of church mice. They were monks in a monastery. They were sleeping giants. Now they have risen.

"You see? You see? *That's* what he thinks of us! He thinks we're MORONS!"

"Don't look at me; I didn't vote for him!"

"This whole rally has been a sham!"

"Could we all just calm down?"

I see Mr. Esposito and my mom note the rapid decline of things and begin searching the crowd for Enzo and me.

"Quick, before our parents haul us out of here," I say, pulling on Enzo, but he's pulling in a different direction.

"They're on the move!" he shouts over the raging crowd, and I look to where he's pointing just in time to see Gordon Cleave and Officer Tapps disappear into the trees.

"This is it!" I say. "You're sure Maritza and Trinity are in position at the Observatory?"

"Positive!"

"They really *are* clueless!" I say to Enzo, probably looking a smidge wild-eyed, but it's impossible not to.

"Aaron," I hear Mya's voice say, but I can't seem to stop myself.

"I wasn't sure it was going to work until now. I didn't actually believe it. But they're going to perform the ceremony! They're going to use a fake device! It isn't going to work, and Trinity and Mya are going to catch them, and the entire town is here to see them crash and burn!"

"Aaron!" I hear Mya insist from somewhere behind me, and I hadn't realized she'd wandered from my side in all the confusion.

But when I turn, I understand the panic in her voice. There's my dad, looking down at me, then at Enzo, then at me again. Enzo looks petrified, and so does Mya.

I might, too, except . . . *Dad* looks just as petrified.

"Aaron," he says, his voice deep and low and cutting straight through the agitated crowd. "What have you done?"

But for the first time in as long as I can remember, I'm not afraid. It's all finally coming to an end, and when it does, I'll have rid our family of the curse of bad fortune. Now we have possession of the device. Or maybe Norman Darby does. Either way, we're going to expose the Ravens, and people will finally understand that the Petersons aren't criminals— arsonists, murderers, mad scientists. We've only ever been simply and horribly unlucky.

"Dad, it's okay. It's all gonna be okay. I made a fake, remember?"

Dad's eyes grow wider, and I want to believe that's his awe at my ingenuity. I want to believe that.

"You . . . were telling me the truth?" Dad asks, and I'd be offended, but I've lied so much, of course he didn't believe me.

Dad doesn't wait for an answer before rushing to the next question, his voice filling with more and more fear.

"You didn't take the device from my office?"

"No, we left it for Gordon Cleave to steal. Your fake was even better than ours, and—"

"What you're telling me is that the device you gave me wasn't the device from my office?"

My stomach keeps sinking because I know I'm not giving him the answers he wants, but I can't understand what he's getting at, and why does my dad look like the world is coming to an end?

"No," I say carefully. "I gave you our device. The one with the missing piece. We thought it'd be safer with you."

"Aaron, we've made a horrible mistake," my dad says.

Even if I knew what to say, I'm not sure I could get the words around the massive knot forming in my throat to match the massive knot that's just dropped in my stomach.

But I do manage to get some words out.

"Where did you go last night?"

"To meet Norman Darby," Dad says, choosing a strange time to be suddenly forthcoming.

"What?" Mya says, and we're doing our best to put it all together, but Enzo is tugging on my shirt.

"They're getting away!" he says. "Maritza and Trinity might need our help!"

But I can't tear away from this awful picture that's forming.

"You figured out the crosswords in the paper," I say. It's like Dad and I are channeling our entire conversation between wild, wide eyes.

"Once I found your name in the letters, I knew. I knew why he'd asked for you. Ike saw it coming even before I did. He knew you'd become a part of this. So I sent my own messages to Darby. I was only trying to protect you, to protect all of us. I tried to keep you from it, Aaron. I tried to keep you and Mya away from all of it!"

Dad is pleading with us to understand. The ciphers, the codes, those were all his. He found his own way to Norman Darby.

"The device we found in your office . . . it wasn't a fake, was it?" I ask. I've never wanted an answer less than I do in this moment.

But there's no time for Dad to lie. "Ike found the pieces of the device my parents buried in the forest. He found them when ground broke on the park."

In a flash, Norman Darby's words come back to me: *To this day, I have no idea what happened to the device they did find. All I know is that they didn't have it when they died. They made sure of that.*

"They couldn't destroy it," I breathe. Of course they couldn't. They didn't know what effect that might have on the balance. So they took it apart and buried the pieces, hid them away with the hope they'd never be found.

Then Ike Gershowitz found them.

"But . . . how did you get the pieces of the device?" I say.

Dad stares at me as the crowd rages around us. I can hear Enzo somewhere behind me, pleading with me to follow. But I can't. Not yet.

"The wallet."

Dad doesn't nod. He doesn't say anything. He doesn't have to.

Ike Gershowitz hid the pieces of the device in the folds of his wallet. And when Dad found them after I was pulled from the tunnels unconscious, he took the wallet to protect the pieces. And once he put them back together, he gave the device to Norman Darby for safekeeping.

He *thought* he gave the device to Norman Darby.

"I didn't know! Dad, I swear, I didn't know!"

"*We* didn't know," Mya says. But it was me. We both know it was really me.

It was me, and it was Dad. In all our efforts to contain the curse, we've managed to unleash it, and now our family is doomed.

"Aaron, I'm going!" Enzo screams over the crowd, and without waiting a second longer, he's off in the direction of the Observatory to assist his sister and Trinity.

"Enzo, no!" my dad shouts, but it's no use.

"Come on," I say, and it's just as useless for my dad to try to stop Mya and me. The only thing he can do is run with us.

Which is exactly what he does.

He easily overtakes the three of us, crashing through the trees like a human bulldozer, swatting branches and parting shrubs, traversing the overgrown path with such ease, it leaves zero doubt that he's been haunting these woods for much longer than we have.

I want so badly to believe it won't matter if the device is real or fake. I want so badly to believe that once they're caught on camera, the Ravens will see justice. But with the actual devices in hand, fortune will always fall in their favor. Proof is irrelevant.

The weight in my stomach and the knot in my throat are threatening to suffocate me, and I wish I could stop running but I can't. I can't until I make this right again.

We've almost made it to the Factory—our entry point into the tunnels—when the distant roar of the angry crowd at the park is replaced by the approaching roar of angry Ravens.

"Get back here, you little brats!"

Suddenly, Maritza and Trinity come bursting through the trees ahead, stopping only when they see my dad. Maritza still screams like she's seen a monster, though. She's staring right up at my dad.

"Get away from my sister!" Enzo shouts and pulls Maritza behind him.

"Enzo, what the—?" But Enzo doesn't let me finish.

"Do you know what he said to her? When she was just trying to go to the bathroom?" Enzo looks angry. I've never seen the way his vein juts out, just like his own dad's. "He said he made Lucy *fly*. Just like an angel. He said he made her *fly*."

I turn to my dad, who can only open his mouth and close it like a fish, like he's gulping for the right words.

"Why would you say that?" I say.

"I . . . I wasn't in my right mind," Dad says feebly.

But clearly the damage is done.

And the damage just keeps coming because seconds later, a cloaked Gordon Cleave and Officer Tapps burst through the brush, looking suddenly ridiculous in their ritual robes, dead leaves sticking to their shiny black feathers.

Trinity backs away from them and takes cover behind my dad, her camera clutched tightly in her hands.

"Just hand over the camera, and we can forget any of this even happened," Gordon Cleave says through gritted teeth.

As though punctuating his threat, lightning fractures the sky, opening the clouds to let the thunder roll through.

"Step back," Dad says, and at first, it works, and Cleave and Tapps take a step back from his impressive mass.

Then Gordon Cleave smirks and lets loose a humorless laugh.

"Or what, Peterson? You'll make us ride one of your death machines?" Cleave inches closer. "It's too late, Peterson. Your fate's already sealed. It's time to accept your lot in life."

"Not after we expose you for the crooks you are!" Trinity says in the biggest voice she can muster, and Dad scoots her back behind him.

"You still don't get it, do you?" Officer Tapps says. "There won't be any charges. There won't be any consequences. That's how this fortune thing works. Things always come up roses for us, one way or another. Now, you can be the weed we pluck from the garden—*or* you can tend the roses. It's your choice."

"Just hand over the camera," Cleave repeats, "and maybe we'll forget this whole night ever happened. Maybe you won't wind up like your friend and his pathetic family."

That's when Trinity aims her camera like a weapon.

And shoots.

Cleave lunges for her. Tapps tries to hold him back. Dad rushes forward to meet Cleave's grasp with a fist.

Maritza and Mya yell Trinity's name. Enzo yells Maritza's name.

And I . . . just stand there. I stand at the edge of the path and watch it all come apart. I should have known I wasn't close to fixing anything. I should have known.

And then . . .

"Is that smoke?" I say, my eyes burning at the gray blur approaching us. The smell is unmistakable.

It's the smell of burning.

It's like I hit the pause button on a movie. Everyone stops to assess the air. Everyone forgets devices and curses and Ravens and crows, and suddenly, we are all animals, relying on instinct.

We're animals trapped in a forest fire.

The screaming from the Golden Apple Amusement Park gains clarity with the thickening of the smoke.

Enzo pulls his shirt collar over his mouth and nose, and the rest of us follow suit.

"Come on," Officer Tapps yells to Gordon Cleave, but Cleave yanks his arm from Tapps's grip. "Not without that film!"

"The smoke's gonna ruin it anyway!" Tapps says. "Besides, do you want to stay and get cooked? Come on!"

"But—" Gordon Cleave objects, his feet dug into the path.

We all start to cough harder.

"Fine," Tapps says. "Stay here and choke. I'm gone."

It wasn't an empty threat. The brave Raven Brooks officer turns tail and flees in the opposite direction, leaving the rest of us to fend for ourselves.

Gordon Cleave squints his eyes and hisses, "This isn't over." And he bounds off in the same direction as Tapps.

Dad turns to the rest of us, particularly Mya and me.

"Head toward the Weather Station. There's a path out of the forest from there."

"It's faster through the tunnels," I object.

"No! It's far too dangerous," Dad says, holding me by the shoulders. "They aren't stable enough. If the fire gets too hot, they could collapse. Stay *out* of the tunnels!"

"Where are you going?" Mya asks, close to tears.

"I have to go back and find your mother," Dad says.

There he is. There's Dad. The Dad I've waited months to see—not just the one that is there for a fleeting second, the one who's here, really, truly, here. I take a long, hard look at him— his crinkled face and dancing eyes, his arms flexed to protect, his gruff voice too full of love to sound scary. I'm happy, but I also have a horrible feeling this is the last time I'll ever see this Dad again. Even if he and Mom make it out okay.

Then he's gone, disappearing into the smoke that has quickly overtaken us.

"Come on!" I holler, backing us out of the thick air and finding a place for us to breathe easier.

Trinity surprises me by turning in the direction of the Factory instead.

"We have to get back to the Observatory," she says.

"Are you out of your mind?" I say. The sudden role reversal of Trinity as the irresponsible one and me as the voice of reason is even more disorienting than the smoke.

"The device," she says. "I know it's real. I knew there had to be a mix-up. They started the ceremony. It was working, just like the rest of the devices," she says.

Then tears start to streak her smoke-stained face. "I must have made a noise when I saw it. That's how we got caught."

I shake my head. "It's all my fault, Trinity. I'm the reason it all got messed up. Besides, Cleave has the real device. There's no point in going back into the tunnels."

"Cleave doesn't have the device," Maritza says meekly from behind her brother, who is looking at me like the monster he believes my dad is.

"What do you mean?" says Mya.

Maritza doesn't want to part with the secret, though. "Aaron, just do what your dad said."

"Maritza, what did you mean?"

"Cleave kinda . . . chucked it at my head," Maritza says. "When they heard us."

"What?"

"It's still in there somewhere," Maritza says.

Mya looks at me. "Aaron, no! You heard what Dad said."

"I have to try," I say, my mind already made up. "This is my last shot at making it right. Promise me you'll head for the Weather Station like Dad said."

"Aaron—!" Mya shouts, but she's already a distant voice.

I think for the briefest of seconds that I might hear a thunder of footsteps behind me. I hadn't realized there was any hope of friendship left in me, but there I was, hoping for backup. Hoping for someone at my side.

But my dad made a horrible confession to Maritza, and Maritza told Enzo, and Enzo told Trinity, and this fragile link that had been holding us together for so long finally broke.

I fly through the trees and out the small opening in the path that clears for the Factory. I flinch, half expecting Cleave or Tapps to lunge at me from either side of the tree line, but neither of them is anywhere to be found.

Cowards to the end, I think, knowing that what I'm doing isn't so much courageous as incredibly stupid, but I have to.

I have to.

I yank the Factory basement door open, which is mercifully unlocked, and stumble down the steps and past the chair where I found and solved the crossword to discover Norman Darby's hidden message to me.

Because I was supposed to be our family's last hope.

You're a Peterson. This is your family's legacy.

I dart across the basement and through the door leading farther down, all the way to the tunnels.

They're already filling with smoke.

I gasp for air, but the running is only making it worse, and soon, my throat is burning and my eyes are watering so much, I can barely see.

I run as fast as my legs will carry me, but it's like every bone in my body is petrifying with each step. I'm feeling nauseated from the smoke that must have traveled far beyond the Golden Apple Amusement Park and made its way into the Weather Station, through the passage by Grandma and Grandpa's office and into the tunnels.

I run with every ounce of strength I have left in me, but that's barely anything. The smoke is filling the tunnels, is filling me. I can't see six inches in front of me, and every breath I take turns into a long, gasping cough.

"Come on," I choke, but it's no use. I have no choice but to drop to the ground here. If I thought I'd find relief this low, though, I was wrong.

But I have to try. I have to try.

The device is somewhere in here, and I can still turn this around. I can still change our family's fortune.

The tunnel is beginning to spin around me, turning right side up and upside down as I drag my body through the grime.

I'm so close. I must be.

I pull my body, but my arms are too weak.

Just a little farther.

But what was smoky and distorted is now gray.

I have to make it right.

Now charcoal.

I have to try.

Then the world goes dark.

CHAPTER 13

Everything hurts, from my eyes against the dimly lit room to the scorch in my throat to the throbbing in my head.

What I see is a room I've seen before.

I was in the tunnels. Just like last time right before I woke up in the hospital.

Unlike last time, though, Mom is with me.

"Dad—"

"Is home with Mya," Mom says, her hand covering mine on the mattress. "They're safe. Everyone is safe. Your friends and their parents, too."

Your friends.

"Who found me?" I say, and I know it's the wrong question, but I have no idea what the right one is.

Mom stares hard at me.

"I don't know," she says quietly.

"Did I have anything?" I say.

"What?"

"Was I holding anything?"

"Aaron," she says, looking hard at me, then over her shoulder as she considers flagging down the nearest nurse.

She turns back, pressing her hand a little tighter over mine, like she wants to keep me from floating away.

"The only thing you were hanging on to in that tunnel was your life." Her voice breaks. "And you barely got out with that."

"They're gone, aren't they?" I say. "The tunnels."

I brace for the answer.

"The walls crumbled in. Whatever was there has been filled in by rubble," she says quietly.

I swallow, absorbing every ounce of pain it creates. I deserve that. I've doomed our family. The device is gone. Buried in the rubble. Sealed in like a tomb.

Sealed just like our family's curse.

"I won't ask why you were there," Mom says. "I know I should ask. Maybe a better mother would. But there will be time for all of that later. Right now, you need your rest."

I close my eyes against the reality of the room and the hospital and all that's transpired, and when I can only hear the beep of the machine, and only feel the tug of the IV needle, I can almost convince myself that this summer never happened. I only thought I woke up that first time, and this has all been a dream. I'll wake up now, and I'll have it to do all over again. I'll never become the Puzzle Master's assistant, I'll never make a decoy device.

Maybe I can go back further.

I'll never find Gordon Cleave's device in the nest, never learn the real identity of the Forest Protectors that haunt the woods occupied by the Golden Apple Corporation. I'll never find the

Weather Station, or my grandparents' notebooks. I'll never find the tunnels.

And most of all, Dad will never build the Golden Apple Amusement Park, and Lucy will live, and Ike Gershowitz will live, and my friends won't fear me like they fear my dad. There will be nothing to fear. The Petersons never moved to Raven Brooks.

* * *

Mya sleeps at the foot of my bunk that night. I tried to tell her not to, but she wouldn't hear it.

"I'm the reason," I say to her after guessing she hadn't fallen asleep. The house is quiet, like it's waiting for the next horrible thing to happen.

"Reason for what?" she says carefully.

"I'm the reason for the curse."

"Aaron, the Ravens are the reason. They're the ones who ruined the balance. Besides, with them exposed now, we'll see how much of this was really bad luck, and how much was them trying to stop us from finding them out." Mya sits up. "You are not the curse."

It's pointless to argue. She'll keep saying I'm not, but I know I am. The balance is off now. It's off for good.

"Even Norman Darby didn't know what would happen if the balance in fortune shifted," Mya says, guessing my thoughts. "None of us can really know, least of all you."

But she's wrong. I can't say why; it's just something I feel in my bones, something so natural, it's like the truth beats right next to my heart, breathes right next to my lungs.

I'm the curse.

"Nobody knows the real power of those devices, Aaron. Or the rituals, or the storms. Not even the Ravens really knew what they were doing."

Mya is trying to comfort me, and with everything I have, I want to believe her. I'm aching to believe her.

But I remember the strange strength of those bony hands that grasped my shoulders in that tunnel and pulled me to safety in the grass. I remember the frantic paranoia in the words Norman Darby spoke to me right before he left me for the paramedics to find.

It's up to you now, Aaron is what Norman Darby said to me before retreating again into hiding. *Your family's fate lies in your hands. Protect them. They'll need it.*

"Try to get some sleep," Mya says before drifting off and leaving me awake.

I'll try, Mya. I'll try.

But I already know that from now on, sleep is going to allude me. Rest won't come easily. What's that saying? *No rest for the wicked?*

I guess that's true. *No rest for the wicked.*

No rest for the cursed. And the cursed is me.

EPILOGUE

Six Months Later.

Miguel Esposito takes a deep breath through his nose.

"I love the smell of printing ink in the morning," he says.

His long-trusted editor haunts his desk, leaning these days more than standing. Ed is getting old.

"Miguel, I thought I loved the news. Then I met you. You ruined all that for me."

The men laugh, the old joke between them never really growing tired. Miguel drives his team hard, his faithful editors grumble, and they all get the newspaper out on time. Every day.

The newsroom is a little slower these days. Not as slow as during Channel Four's heyday, but Channel Seven's down-home charm has caught on. Miguel sighs. Raven Brooks seems destined to be a television news–first town, no matter how hard he tries.

He can't complain, though. The news is still plentiful—there's enough to go around, especially here.

Ed hands him the lead story:

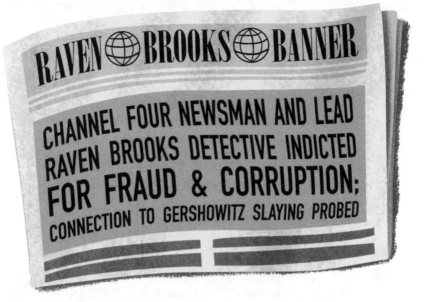

RAVEN ⊕ BROOKS ⊕ BANNER

CHANNEL FOUR NEWSMAN AND LEAD RAVEN BROOKS DETECTIVE INDICTED FOR FRAUD & CORRUPTION;
CONNECTION TO GERSHOWITZ SLAYING PROBED

"Above the fold," Miguel says.

It's good to see Gordon Cleave and Dale Tapps get what's coming to them. After all that business with those underground rituals and dressing in feathers. Miguel stifles another shiver as he pushes the thought away. He's not sure anyone could have seen that one coming.

Well, almost no one. Rita Ryland knew something, that's for sure.

And the Petersons. It seems the Peterson family is never far from his mind anymore, as much as he'd like for it to be.

"I heard Chet Biggs went over to Redmond's twenty-four-hour news network," Ed says.

"Good. They can keep him," Miguel smirks.

He pulls up the next story, placing the copy on the proof page like a puzzle piece fitting into place:

GOLDEN APPLE AMUSEMENT PARK FIRE
INVESTIGATION CONTINUES; TUNNELS
DEEMED TOO UNSTABLE TO EXPLORE

Miguel's stomach clenches. He can't remember a fear greater than not knowing where Enzo and Maritza were on that day. He's not sure he can ever forgive Peterson for that. And after what he said to Maritza . . .

"I should have protected them better," he mutters.

"What's that, now?" Ed says, leaning his good ear toward his boss.

Miguel shakes his head. "A darn shame," he says. "Brenda Yi deserved better than that horror show."

Ed grunts his agreement as he slides the next story into place along the bottom right of the page:

UNSEATED, BUT NOT UNLOVED; RAVEN BROOKS
FORGIVES THEIR FORMER MAYOR TAVISH

Both men shake their head at that one.

"Some guys have all the luck," Ed says.

Miguel rubs his chin. "We still need to find space for the Golden Apple Corporation bankruptcy story."

Ed pulls on the back of his neck.

"I guess it's too much to ask that Raven Brooks go back to being a sleepy little town," Miguel says, trying to laugh.

Ed looks at him, smiling wryly. "C'mon, Miguel."

"What?"

"It was never a sleepy little town," he says.

The men sink into their chairs, staring at the New Year's Eve edition.

"I'm not coming back next year, Miguel," Ed says after a pause.

Miguel begins to object, but he saw this coming. Ed's done his job well, probably too well; he's going to be impossible to replace.

"I'm never going to find another you," Miguel says to his trusted colleague.

"Nope!" Ed says with a little satisfaction. After another pause, he remembers a name Miguel has brought up here and there.

"How about that fella you used to room with in college? What's his name? Roth?"

Miguel perks up a little. "Jay," he says. "You know what? That's not a bad idea. I might just look him up someday."

The men take in the buzz of activity in the newsroom.

"Admit it, Ed. You're going to miss this."

Ed smiles. "Not a bit. Now instead of reporting on this weird little town, I just get to live in it. Maybe play a few video games with my grandkids."

Miguel sighs. "Welp, guess we've got everything but the Puzzle."

Ed leans toward his friend. "Is it just me, or is that Puzzle Master fella a little . . ." He whistles a little tweet, circling his finger beside his ear.

Miguel shrugs. "Yeah, but the readers love him. What can I say? People love a puzzle they can't solve."

As if on cue, the courier arrives with the top-secret puzzle for tomorrow's special New Year's edition. Miguel carefully breaks the seal.

"Huh. Looks like our Puzzle Master is trying out a new game," Miguel says, and places the content into the square set aside on the Puzzles page. "If I'm up on my terminology, I believe they call this an ambigram."

"Fits perfectly," Ed says.

"Yeah, it always seems to, doesn't it?" says Miguel, transfixed by the new ambigram before him. "Good luck to anyone trying to crack this code."

Dig Deep for the Way Out.

The Red Key Will Set You
Free When

The Time Comes.

Trust Narf.

About the Author

CARLY ANNE WEST is the author of the YA novels *The Murmurings* and *The Bargaining*. She holds an MFA in English and Writing from Mills College and lives with her husband and two kids near Portland, Oregon. Visit her at carlyannewest.com.